HOW TO STEAL THE Mona Lisa

HOW TO STEAL THE Mona Lisa

BETHANY WALKER

Illustrated by **JACK NOEL**

SCHOLASTIC

Published by Scholastic, 2022
Euston House, 24 Eversholt Street, London, NW1 1DB, UK
Scholastic Ireland, 89E Lagan Road, Dublin Industrial Estate,
Glasnevin, Dublin, D11 HP5F

Text © Bethany Walker, 2022
Illustrations © Jack Noel, 2022

ISBN 978 0702 31431 5

Printed by CPI Group (UK) Ltd, Croydon, CR0 4YY
Papers used by Scholastic Children's Books are made
from wood grown in sustainable forests.

1 3 5 7 9 10 8 6 4 2

www.scholastic.co.uk

For all
budding
artists

Dear Granny,

Remind me never to tell Jake Janowski ANYTHING. I doubt
you've heard about our little public demonstration,
but it's been BIG news in Colpepper. I'm still not sure
how I got from being the proud owner of my first pair
of glasses to protesting outside the optician's about MIND-CONTROL SPECS
with Jake, but he had got it into his head about something FISHY going
on with **MC Glasses** and next thing I know, I'm holding placards and

shouting about MIND CONTROL down Colpepper High
Street. I COMPLETELY blame Jake for all this. He was
so convincing about the whole "mind control" thing.
You've got to admire Jake's enthusiasm for his
own loopy theories.

Unsurprisingly, Mum and Dad aren't best
pleased. I did *try* to tell them that the whole thing
was Jake's idea, but they sadly don't see it that way.
They pointed out that Jake did not *force* me to protest and neither did
he *force* me to take off my brand-spanking-new glasses and stamp on

1

them. (You should have seen it, Granny. It was ever so theatrical!) I have to admit, I did get swept up with Jake's theory, but sadly the glasses-stamping did not turn up any evidence of a mind-control device (whatever that   might look like, anyway), and I was left with a mangled mess, which is a major downer as, actually, I rather liked my new glasses.

BUM.

Well, at least I've given Mum and Dad something to agree on, which doesn't happen much these days. In fact, they're in agreement about three things:

- Me and Jake had to make a public apology in the *Colpepper Gazette*, which is all kinds of embarrassing, but maybe I can cope with it for the sake of parental harmony.

- I am grounded, which is fine by me because I will absolutely <u>not</u> be hanging out with Jake **EVER AGAIN** and, following all this humiliation, I'm happy to keep my head down.

- They **WILL NOT** buy me new glasses. How unfair is that? I mean, I know their business isn't doing very well, but surely we can afford a replacement pair of glasses? They seem to be able to afford stuff for SEABERT. Mum gave me the whole "we're not made of money" spiel while Dad went on about me "learning to value" stuff and "thinking before I act" and "stop rolling those eyes at me, young lady".

So I have to save up for them myself - by helping Mum and Dad with their work. BLEURGH! No thanks! I would rather poke my own eyes out than have to undertake such a mind-blastingly, brain-numbingly pointless activity as having anything to do with the endless instructions that Mum and Dad write for alarm systems.

Instead, I was hoping, oh Granny dearest, sweet Granny, oh favourite granny of mine, that you might see your way to BUYING ME SOME NEW GLASSES. Here are some very good reasons why:

1. As a budding artist, my eyesight is MASSIVELY important to me. For the short amount of time I had them, those glasses were like magic. Trees had ACTUAL LEAVES on them, not just green blurry blobs. And people had faces, with eyebrows and everything. Wearing glasses was like being given SUPER VISION! Now, I know you're going to write back and go on and on about Monet and his bad eyesight and the fact that he invented Impressionism, which I agree totally rocks, but he was, like, a **THOUSAND** when he painted those pictures. Surely, as an art enthusiast yourself, you wouldn't want to deny your dear, darling granddaughter the opportunity to reach for greatness, to fulfil her potential, to meet her artistic destiny?

2. Even though you SAID you'd be visiting soon, I know something will come up and you won't be able to make it, LIKE ALWAYS. Buying me new glasses could help me cope with the DISAPPOINTMENT of not seeing you.

3. You have spent many years building up your reputation for buying me all the best gifts - thanks again for this awesome DoodlePadX500 for our emails. Surely you don't want someone **else** to get me new glasses?

DOODLEPAD
x500

4. And, speaking of gifts, Jake only developed his crazed "mind-controlling glasses" theory after you sent him *that* book for his birthday, which he totally took as a sign that something was up with MC Glasses and not just A MASSIVE COINCIDENCE. Once Jake got a sniff of a conspiracy theory, this was never going to play out any other way. It was really sweet of you to send a present to my best friend*, but it basically means the blame for this whole situation lands at your feet. So you DEFINITELY should buy me some new glasses.

How are those for some **compelling** reasons?

So can you send me some new glasses? Please? Surely you can find an optician in whatever fabulous and fancy place you're currently visiting?

It's so unfair. You're swanning around wherever, and I'm stuck here at home with barely-talking-to-each-other parents. Even going to Mum's favourite place in the world – you know, the Deep – doesn't seem to cheer them up any more. We went yesterday, but, thanks to having NO GLASSES, the fish were all just blurry blobs. I even thought I saw a woman swimming in a flowery dress in one of the tanks – how ludicrous would that have been? Stupid rubbish eyesight! Normally I'd have tried to persuade them to take me to an art gallery (not that that's ever been successful, but there has to be a first time, right?), but there wasn't even any point this time as I can't actually SEE anything. Is it fair that we *always* get to do what Mum and Dad want to do (actually, make that Mum, Dad and SEABERT – we can't forget their beloved, super, amazing, incredible *STARFISH*), but <u>never</u> anything I want to do?

   At least school is starting next week. I can't believe I'm finally going to secondary school. After all the stuff you told me about when you were a pupil at Colpepper Hall School, I can't wait to get started. I am going to be the best artist the school will have ever produced! Just so long as I can see. (HINT HINT.) Write back soon!

Love, *Mia*

* Correction: Jake WAS my best friend. I'm never going to listen to his moronic theories again! New school = new friends.

PS I suppose you'll want to see my fifteen minutes of ~~fame~~ humiliation... Here's a scan of my and Jake's apology. As Jake's parents are the owners of the newspaper, you'd have thought they'd hide the apology somewhere right at the bottom, but NOOOOOO, we were the headline news! And did they *have* to include a photo? Thanks for nothing, Mr and Mrs Janowski!

A PUBLIC APOLOGY FROM MIA BERGHLER AND JAKE JANOWSKI

Mia Berghler and Jake Janowski would like to apologize for any offence and reputational damage caused to Mr Michael Chimaera of MC Glasses, 22 High Street, Colpepper.

"Mr Michael Chimaera is a fully trained and professional optician and he is not, in any way, shape or form, involved in the **mind control** of the vast number of customers he serves. He is well respected in the town of Colpepper, not just as an optician but also as the local Member of Parliament (MP). The name of his business, 'MC Glasses', relates purely to his initials, not mind control as we suggested during our protest held outside his shop in Colpepper town centre on August 23rd.

"We apologize without reservation and would like to thank Mr Chimaera for taking the time to show us the many certificates proving his qualifications, and are also grateful for the demonstration of the optometric devices he uses. We now know that it was purely coincidental that there was a striking resemblance between the Optic Trial Lens Frame, used by Mr Chimaera to measure the strength of each eye, and the device used in the popular *fictional* book about mind control by author TC Kingston, *Banana Smoothies, Mind Control Specs and Steve.*"

Mia Berghler would also like to thank Mr Chimaera for agreeing to provide replacement glasses for her, once she has the funds to purchase them.

"I have learned that I should not stamp on glasses, and I should warn other people not to stamp on their glasses either," said Mia Berghler. "It is a silly thing to do

...FOUND

anyone missing a chameleon? ...und in Colpepper Town Square. ...cm long and is blue or green or ...k, or basically any colour. If you ...ink this is your chameleon, then ...ntact this paper.

...OCAL SCHOOL ...UILDING AT RISK

...olpepper Hall, the building that ...ouses Colpepper Hall School, is ...rumbling after years of underfunding ...nd neglect. Unless funds are found to ...save the east wing, the only option will ...be to demolish that part of the school.

Colpepper Hall was originally built over two-hundred years ago by the town's beloved founder, Lord Colpepper. Once an opulent residence, the building fell into disrepair as Lord Colpepper's fortune dwindled. The contents of the property were sold off following Lord Colpepper's death and the property was finally turned into a school after standing empty for several decades.

If the east wing is demolished, it's not all bad news, as it would allow space for a much-needed car park.

GOVERNMENT THREATENING FURTHER CUTS TO ART EDUCATION

Since the government cut the budget for art education at universities by 50% last year, fewer young people have been able to take up places to study the arts beyond secondary school. For this reason, the government is considering whether there is any point in children studying the arts between the ages of eleven and sixteen either, when they should be focusing their time on more important subjects.

A government spokesperson issued this statement: "We must acknowledge that, despite the huge wealth generated in this country by our cultural heritage sites, dynamic performing arts and talented visual artists, what school pupils need to focus on is achieving high grades in maths, English and science: subjects that will be useful for future careers in business, industry and finance. Who really wants to be an artist or musician anyway? By removing artistic education for these pupils, we are actually *helping* direct them to more achievable goals."

If agreed, the funding cuts would come into place from the new year.

J,

GO AWAY! I'm not talking to you,

and you are no longer my friend.

Find someone else to tell your ridiculous

conspiracy theories to.

And I **DON'T** need you acting as my

guide dog.

M

From: MiaB@StarfishInstructions.net   ≡ ×
To: KBerg55@fjsn.net
Date: 3 September
Subject: THE WORST POSSIBLE START TO SCHOOL

Dear Granny,

How can a day start off with so much sunny promise and quickly become a pit of despair and terribleness?

I can't even bear to describe to you how excited I was to put on my new uniform, especially with my cheeky artistic addition of a beret and smock – not strictly part of the official uniform, but even though I'm still without any glasses (did you get my last email, by the way?) I didn't need to see myself in a mirror to know that *I looked awesome*. My choice of uniform was my way of ANNOUNCING the arrival of the NEW, GREAT ARTIST at Colpepper Hall School – me – but, instead, as soon as I arrived at school, we were all rushed into an emergency assembly and I was AMBUSHED by a totally different announcement:

The art department has officially been shut down!

That's it.

There are no art lessons.

No art teacher.

No art equipment.

And no way for me to become the amazing artist I want to be.

Can you believe it?

According to Mr Scales, the head, it's a double whammy of poop:

- The art department is housed in the east wing of the school, and apparently it's "unsafe" and "dangerous", and it would be "criminally irresponsible to let children into it". Pah! Is that even a reason? Surely artists are supposed to SUFFER for their art? Mr Scales said he's *trying* to think up plans to save the department, but the school governors want it to be bulldozed and used for a car park. WHAT? How can my dreams of becoming an artist be RUINED so Colpepper can get a new car park? I thought it was going to be SO GREAT going to school in an old, beautiful building like Colpepper Hall, but it's turning out to be THE WORST.

- He also said that the GOVERNMENT now wants to cut funding for arts education at schools because there's no point in children really enjoying art and creativity now when they won't be able to do it anyway when they're older. So even if I could transfer schools, there still wouldn't be art lessons! He said we may as well just focus on maths and science and IMPORTANT subjects like that.

IMPORTANT?

IMPORTANT?

Why is art not *important*?

To be fair to Mr Scales, he did *sound* quite upset about the announcement. Maybe he also looked upset too – but I wouldn't know! He said it would basically take a MIRACLE to fix the situation. Then he finished off the assembly as he apparently always does, with the whole school chanting the school motto, <u>**"Success is at our fingertips"**</u>, which felt a bit cruel, considering my best shot at success – an art career – is now no longer at my fingertips, or even within an arm's reach. Nor is it within a stone's throw, and it cannot even be prodded by a bargepole. My artistic success has disappeared off over the horizon. Bye-bye, future.

At least YOU will understand why I'm sad about this. You're the one person who can understand how devastating this news is to me. I tried to talk to Mum and Dad about this after school but they see it as a **"good thing"**, not to be **"wasting my time"** with art. How rubbish is that? So I can't imagine they're going to help make up for the whole NO ART AT SCHOOL thing by, oh, I don't know, suddenly taking me to galleries or anything like that. This is just the WORST news ever.

After the assembly, I was so caught up in my thoughts about the art department that I totally lost track of any of my classmates. And it's not easy trying to find your way around an unknown location when everything is all fuzzy. I found myself in the school's central Dome Area and at last spotted someone to ask for directions, but they didn't acknowledge me, no matter how loudly I spoke. They didn't even look at me. SO RUDE. But maybe they were just as shocked as me by the bombshell news about the art department because they were VERY PALE and STATUE-STILL.

No thanks to them, I eventually found what I *thought* to be the right classroom. NOPE. Let me tell you, sitting for an hour in the wrong class is NO FUN, especially when that wrong class happens to be a year ten maths lesson with a scary maths teacher barking questions at everyone. Each time the teacher shouted, "That question was to you, beret girl," my answers became more and more panicked: "One!" (could have been a lucky guess), "Zero!" (ditto), "Negative!", "Pi!", "Sausages!", "Parachute!". Things did not improve at lunchtime, either, when I served myself what I hoped was vanilla sponge and chocolate sauce for lunch but was actually vanilla sponge and gravy, which do NOT go together.

In the afternoon, Jake tried to guide me around, but I am still NOT TALKING TO HIM and definitely DO NOT WANT HIS HELP. I cannot be associated with Jake if I want to make sensible, non-conspiracy-theory-believing friends. So *HE* needs to get it into his head that we are not friends. To make my point, I flounced away from him in a very dramatic fashion, my smock all swishy and swooshy behind me - artists' smocks are basically designed for flouncing, I've discovered! Unfortunately, I had flounced straight into the boys' toilets. I ended up sitting in there listening to boys widdling for the ENTIRE break because I was too embarrassed to leave the cubicle. MEGA GROSS!

At the end of the day, I thought maybe things were looking up when I spotted Mum waiting for me outside the gate, which was completely unexpected and, to be honest, completely out of character. I rushed to give her a hug. Turns out it was a year eleven called Brianna who, I now know, does not like hugs.

Or year sevens.

Or people called Mia.

Please write back soon – and I'm keeping my fingers crossed about that new pair of glasses I asked for. I clearly need them!

Love,

A very depressed _Mia_

_____

Dearest Mia,

Thank you for your emails. Sorry it's taken a while to get back to you. You know me – here, there and everywhere with my work! Right now I'm in Tokyo, finishing off an in-depth article on studies into the effects of earthquakes titled *Groundbreaking Research on Earthquakes Really Shakes Things Up*.

It feels like the end of the world to you, that announcement about the art department, I know. But your last email showed that you have the most important thing you need for art: passion! If you really want to be an artist, you will find a way. And although I'm not with you in person, I am here for you and I will help in whatever way I can to turn your artistic dreams into reality.

Forget about MC Glasses, won't you? Who wants to shop at the same place as everyone else, anyway? You'll be pleased to hear I've popped some new specs in the post for you and they'll certainly help you stand out from the crowd. Do you know, I used to go to school with Michael Chimaera? He was a pompous bottom even back then, so I'm certain a little protest about his glasses won't have done any damage. Yes, your protest perhaps wasn't the right approach, but it is wonderful to stand up for what you believe in, you know. Anyway, who cares about the nonsense written in the *Colpepper Gazette*? I feel sorry for Jake. I can't believe his parents published the apology and chose to keep the local big-wig happy rather than support their own son. Thankfully, most of us serious journalists have higher standards! Jake clearly has very sensitive instincts, so don't be too hard on him. Do you really want your long friendship ruined by one ill-advised event?

I do hope things improve at school for you. I bet it's very different now from when I attended it. Is the bust of Lord Colpepper still in the Dome Area? In my day, everyone used to rub his nose for luck before exams.

Sorry to hear about your parents not getting on. If their business is in trouble, no wonder they're stressed. But I've learned over the years that they would not be at all happy for me to interfere. I have planned an extensive schedule of activities and articles to write over the next few months, so I'm afraid I wouldn't be able to visit anyway. But don't worry! Things have a way of working themselves out one way or another. You'll see (or you will once the specs arrive – ha!).

So excited, I am. Lance Ling is taking me to a sushi-making workshop so I must go. I'll write again soon. XXX

Kat B. | Freelance journalist for science and nature | fjsn.net
Sent from my phone

£25 MILLION REWARD ANNOUNCED FOR RETURN OF WORLD'S MOST FAMOUS MISSING PAINTING

By Gerta Lowdaviss
The Daily News

Royal Family Offers Huge Reward After Newly Discovered Clue Gives Hope Painting Still Exists

The royal family today announced a £25 million reward for their most famous stolen painting, *The Lost Mona Lisa*, as it has become known. Painted by Leonardo da Vinci c.1505, *The Mona Lisa* is the world's most famous – and most valuable – painting. As was common at the time, the artist painted two versions: one that now lives in the Louvre Museum in France and one that belongs to the British royal family. In 1822, the royal family's version of the painting was stolen from the palace walls during a Christmas party hosted by King George IV in what many people describe as "The Greatest Art Heist of All Time". There have been no leads or clues regarding the painting's whereabouts for almost two hundred years – until now.

In the announcement, a spokesperson for the palace said,

"The royal family has received reliable intelligence regarding the continued existence of their much-beloved and much-missed painting, *The Lost Mona Lisa*. Prompted by this, they are pleased to announce a £25 million reward for the painting's return to its rightful place." It is hoped the huge reward announced today will help solve the mystery of the painting's disappearance once and for all.

The reward is only being offered for a short time, with the intention of spurring people to action and getting the painting back to the Royal Collection in time for the two-hundredth anniversary of the theft. Between now and Christmas, if the painting is found and returned, some lucky person could receive the £25 million finder's fee. But the offered reward expires at Christmas, so don't wait till Boxing Day to empty your attics, dig around your basements, search under your beds or ferret behind your sofas! However small the chance, isn't it worth pursuing for £25 million?

View comments

Related Topics

| Art | Royal Family | Mona Lisa | Culture |

Dear Granny,

Is this a joke?

The parcel arrived. The prescription is spot on, and they feel very comfortable.

HOWEVER ... (and it's a big **HOWEVER**), they look like this:

Not wanting to sound ungrateful or anything, but I LOOK LIKE A COMPLETE WEIRDO. What eleven-year-old would wear these glasses? Standing out from the crowd? That's putting it mildly! After the MC Glasses situation, the last thing I want people to be thinking about when they see me is ... glasses! However, as my attempts to navigate school without glasses did NOT meet with success, I am forced to ...

WEAR THE GLASSES.

Who is Dame Edna Everage?

My new form teacher, Mr Rothering, who clearly thinks he's dead funny, called me that name. Judging by the smirk on his face, it was NOT a compliment. Thankfully, no one else in class seemed to know who this

18

Dame Edna person is either, so it was a wasted reference - ha! However, being called "Dame Edna" is probably preferable to being called "Urinal Girl", which I have been called since someone saw me sneak out of the boys' toilet on the first day. Not a great start to secondary school! I can't tell whether people are sniggering about the toilet incident or my glasses, but I hope you're right that people will forget about these things soon.

But, now I have glasses, I can at least make my way around school properly. I bet this place was amazing when it was Lord Colpepper's home - but now the walls are crumbling and peeling, the corridors echo with kids screeching and teachers shouting, and the whole place smells of overboiled cabbage and boys' toilets. (I wish I could forget how the boys' toilets smell!) You'll be pleased to hear that the bust of Lord Colpepper is still in the Dome Area, although its nose is rather rubbed down and shiny. "Success

is at our fingertips" is carved around the base of the bust, which struck me as odd because a bust is a statue of someone's head and shoulders - there are no fingertips! The bust is in exactly the same place as that rude pupil who wouldn't give me directions on my first day. Unless

I was actually talking to the...

Oh well, never mind.

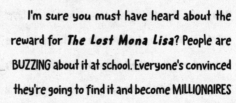

I'm sure you must have heard about the reward for *The Lost Mona Lisa*? People are BUZZING about it at school. Everyone's convinced they're going to find it and become MILLIONAIRES

– as if anyone from *Colpepper*, of all places, will just *happen* across the world's most famous missing painting! In today's assembly, the resident year seven clever-clogs, Arthur Penty, shouted out, "Maybe the school could find *The Lost Mona Lisa*, and save the east wing!" It made us laugh, but Mr Scales didn't see the funny side of it. Poor man. It would be amazing, though – it would be the MIRACLE that Mr Scales said the school needs.

Most people are searching their homes for the missing painting, but, considering it's been missing for two-hundred years and we live in an open-plan new-build, there's no mathematical possibility that it's hidden in our house. Wouldn't it be funny if someone had just had it hanging on their wall all this time? I'd love ANY painting to be hung on our walls at home – it wouldn't need to be worth 25p, let alone £25 million! The closest we come to having a painting is the huge mural of STARFISH photos, which Mum put up to help SEABERT "feel more at home". And don't forget the diagrams of aquatic creatures or the ENDLESS photos of SEABERT with his many, many rosettes he's won for "Most Amazing Asteroidea", "Biggest Barnacle Eater" and "Purplest Skin".* However, when I've tried to put up *actual* art, even just in my bedroom, Dad's complained about the "frivolous clutter" and taken the pictures down. So unfair!

Just what is my parents' problem with art? How come they hate it when you and I both love it? You'd think that all people could find some form of art that they like, whether it's a very traditional still-life drawing of some fruit or a

splashy-splashy Pollock painting. I know people say that certain traits can skip a generation, like shortness, curly hair or nose-picking (actually, I'm not sure about the nose-picking, but Mum swears she NEVER does it) – but can a love of ART skip a generation? What I really don't get is how you and Dad are related in the first place. You just seem to have nothing in common, so no wonder you don't really get on. Jake's theory about you both (of course Jake has a theory, he ALWAYS has a theory) is that Dad is actually a MASSIVE rebel, only he rebelled by making his life as organized, safe and grey as it is humanly possible to be. As a Jake theory goes, it's actually not bad. **But I won't be telling Jake that – it would only encourage him.**

Love, *Mia*

* Is it normal for parents to have more photos of their pet STARFISH (twenty-seven photos in total around our house at last count) than of their one and only child (two-and-a-half photos, but just because I *happened* to be standing next to Seabert when those pictures were taken)?

Hey M,

Ignore Mr Rothering and our classmates - I think your glasses look cool. And no one's going to be controlling your mind with those on, that's for sure!

JJ

PS Any plans for Saturday?

Dearest Mia,

At the risk of making you cross, do you realize that you complain a lot about your parents not understanding or appreciating your interest in art, while also complaining about their interest in sea creatures? How can you expect them to embrace your interests when you don't embrace theirs? I'm not saying it's fair or right that you feel they prioritize Seabert over you and your interests, but maybe if you just tried a *little*, it would help improve things. Maybe you'd even start having fun together as a family? And while art seems to be off the agenda for you for now, would it be the worst thing to develop other interests?

Funnily enough, even when you're complaining about your parents, you manage to include a comment about Jake. Are you really *sure* that friendship is over? Remember, he always gave you somewhere you could escape from Seabert. Don't you miss your – what did you call them? – Seabert-free Saturday Sleepovers?

I fear I'm to blame for your dad's dislike of art. There was a time when he showed an interest in painting and I thought he'd take after me. Dragged him to all kinds of galleries when he was young, I did. Although that's probably where his interest in electrical systems and alarms comes from; those blasted gallery alarms were always going off during our gallery visits back then. Your father even started taking an umbrella with him whenever we went to a gallery, as the sprinkler systems used to go off on a very regular basis!

Of course I've heard about the reward for *The Lost Mona Lisa*. £25 million is *such* a big reward – certainly more money than I need or I want! To steal the world's most famous painting from the royal family must have been such a daring act two-hundred years ago. Quite a mystery, but someone will surely know something. I just hope the reward will go to someone deserving, don't you?

Right, have to sign off. Have treated myself to a whale-watching cruise after completing my latest article – *Overworked Shark Dentist Admits Biting Off More Than He Can Chew* – and the boat is about to set off from Seattle harbour. I don't want to miss anything. XXX

Kat B. | Freelance journalist for science and nature | fjsn.net
Sent from my phone

To Codename Iris,

This timing is perfect. You are in position at school and the announcement from the royal family means that we will soon be millionaires! I won't even have to bother trying to sell the painting on the black market! All that stands between us and that reward is your simple task of finding five skeleton keys.

Keep your head down. No one can suspect a thing.

Codename Boss Eye

From: MiaB@StarfishInstructions.net   ≡ ×
To: KBerg55@fjsn.net
Date: 11 September
Subject: Starfish-free zone

Dear Granny,

Did you really tell me I should try to *embrace* Mum and Dad's hobby? Really? I don't know how I can do that when I'm so sick of EVERYTHING being about SEABERT, his blasted aquarium and endless visits to sea centres and aquariums. Isn't there more to life than **sea creatures**? I mean, I don't actually mind SEABERT, but it's got to a point where I think my parents' STARFISH obsession is starting to play tricks on my mind.

Last night, I sewed the school logo on to my beret and smock – to make them look more official. (Apparently some pupils had whinged about my very awesome but slightly unauthorized outfit – but surely no one can complain if there's a school logo on it, right?) As I sewed, all I could see in the logo for Colpepper Hall School was a bloomin' STARFISH . SURELY the logo can't really contain a *starfish*? It was really doing my head in, so I asked Mr Rothering this morning, and all he said was, "It's a logo – it doesn't have to *MEAN* anything."

Definitely a starfish!

Unfortunately, Jake heard my question and spent the rest of the day bugging me with his idea of what the five-pointed thing in the middle of the logo could be. I was trying so hard not to listen, but he just kept muttering about it being a hand, and that makes sense because of the school motto, blah, blah, blah. ARGH! Nobody cares what you think, Jake – it just looks like a starfish! But, to be fair, everything starts to look like a starfish when you've grown up with SEABERT.*

So no, I'm NOT going to embrace Mum and Dad's obsession with SEABERT, and we're not suddenly going to start to have fun as a family. What do *they* find fun anyway? I'm not sure my idea of fun is the same as theirs. Like, do they actually find their job " FUN "? Is writing instructions for alarm systems "important"? Probably. Is it interesting, exciting or FUN ?

No.

Nope.

No way.

Nuh-uh.

Nopey-dopey-doo-dah.

Anyway, whether it's fun or not, "Starfish Instructions" is NOT doing well, and it's affecting them in different ways: Mum is just spending more and more time with SEABERT, and Dad spends all his time complaining about his nervous stomach ache – he's even taken to cuddling his old blanket, which is driving Mum nuts. (You remember the one? His fluffy "blanky" covered with fish?) According to Dad, people don't need instructions for alarm equipment

27

any more. There's a whole new generation of "intuitive" products that people just basically have to plug in. He moans ALL THE TIME about the Verisafe Alarm 3000, which, in his mind, is his nemesis and completely to blame for the failings of his beloved Starfish Instructions business.

There may not be anything I can do to help Mum and Dad or Starfish Instructions, but I have been trying to think of things *I* can do at school if I can't do art (and here's a hint for you – it will have NOTHING to do with aquatic creatures). I haven't given up on the art department completely, though. I've decided, next time I get the chance, I'm going to ask Mr Scales if there's something I can do to help him.

Even though the art department is closed, the music department seems to be thriving – maybe because everyone, including the head, is a little bit terrified of the teeny music teacher, Miss Tench. If I was Mr Scales, I wouldn't dare cut her budget either! She came round during tutorial to ask us about playing instruments. Shanice put her hand up and said she already plays the flute. Shanice looks really interesting – and wears glasses that **_really_** suit her, unlike... But I've never spoken to her (actually, I've never seen her speak to anyone in my class).

When I asked about learning an instrument, Miss Tench took one look at my outfit and said I clearly needed something that stood out from the crowd. I'd like to *think* it was a compliment about my awesome arty get-up? Well, she had a point, so I picked the TUBA. I love it! I can only play one note on it so far, but it's so low and grumbly!

If I play it loud enough, the water in Seabert's tank vibrates.

Love, *Mia*

* So, yes, I've mentioned Jake again, but that's because he's really annoying now and it was completely relevant to the point I was making. It's definitely not to do with missing him. At all. Even a little bit.

Hey M,

You didn't seem to hear me trying to tell you...

Look: a hand!

Want a Seabert-less Saturday Sleepover this weekend?
Mum's got Wagon Wheels in!

JJ.

J,

Stop trying to talk to me. **WE ARE NO LONGER FRIENDS.**

I didn't ask your advice, so stop bothering me about hands and fingertips!

GO AWAY.

M

EYE FOR TRUTH

by Jake Janowski

Question: What do you do when your best friend stops listening to you and you have no one to tell all your awesome discoveries to?

Answer: You write them in a blog!

Welcome to Jake Janowski's Blog: **EYE FOR TRUTH**

Now, you might be thinking *Oh no, it's another conspiracy theory blog – enough already!* and I understand your reaction, but, trust me, this is **no conspiracy theory blog**. For starters, as the son of local newspaper editors, I have read my fair share of conspiracy theories, sent in by ... well, I won't name names, but YOU KNOW WHO YOU ARE. Rest assured, I believe the Earth is round, that man DID land on the moon and that Elvis most certainly did pop his clogs while sitting on the toilet back in 1977. In my opinion, it's the *people in power* who continue to spread this NONSENSE just to give real whistle-blowers a bad name. *People in power* don't want you to believe anything except THEIR VERSION OF THE TRUTH – but what is true? Here, in my EYE FOR TRUTH blog, I will seek out and report THE TRUTH. And if you find yourself not believing me, that's only WHAT *THEY* WANT YOU TO THINK!

You might have last seen me in a local news source "apologizing" for offending a local businessman and politician. OK, so there was no actual "evidence" of anything dodgy with that person's business, but I still don't understand why LOADS of recent customers that I contacted complained about headaches and high-pitched noises ... *when wearing their glasses!* You don't even have to take my word for it – read TG Kingston's *Banana Smoothies, Mind-Control Specs and Steve* and your eyes, too, will be opened. And even if my best friend isn't currently speaking to me, I'm pleased to see she hasn't bought a replacement pair from that establishment – and I don't care what anyone else says, I think she looks very cool in her new specs. Take it from me, people – seeing sometimes ISN'T believing, and there's something fishy about ~~MC Glasses~~ that shop.

Speaking of Fishy, did you see all that hoo-ha about the two-hundredth anniversary of the theft of *The Lost Mona Lisa*? How can they possibly call that "<u>The Greatest Art Heist of All Time</u>"? Maybe it was, like, two-hundred years ago, but how can the theft of one measly painting compare to the daring and awesome heists pulled off by that most famous of cat burglars, The Fish?

Have you ever heard of The Fish? No? I'm not surprised. There was a time, ten to fifteen years ago, when you couldn't MOVE for newspaper reports on The Fish. Back then, galleries discovered teeny fish painted somewhere in their paintings: the calling card of The Fish, signalling the painting had been taken and replaced by a fake. The Fish was never caught, and no one ever worked out who they were – but surely they're still around?

Maybe this whole reward thing is part of The Fish's plan to steal it for themselves anyway – it's totally the kind of thing The Fish would do. If anyone is going to find *The Lost Mona Lisa*, it'll be The Fish and, as an admirer of The Fish's skill and daring, I'm going to make it my mission to find out who The Fish is.

Although, the £25 million reward for finding *The Lost Mona Lisa* would be handy for Colpepper Hall School, which seems pretty desperate for money. The art department has been closed down, we've been told, because the east wing of the school is ready to crumble, and my best friend is really sad about it.

BUT why do I keep seeing Mr Scales go in there WITHOUT A HARD HAT? And I've seen him lounging around on the roof.

Are you ready for **EYE FOR TRUTH'S** first big scoop?

I don't think there is anything wrong with the school building.

Think about it a moment. Everyone was going on about how upset Mr Scales looked when he announced the closure – but they weren't really looking properly. Were there tears? No!

What I noticed was weird, dry eyes.

REPTILIAN eyes.

And this got me thinking – is Mr Scales all he seems to be?

Number of views: 5   **Likes: 1**

INTERNATIONAL ESPIONAGE AGENCY

SURVEILLANCE REPORT

KEYWORD MONITORING ALERT

Keyword identified: The Fish

Alert level: Low

Action required: None

MONA LISA MAGIC

By Gerta Lowdaviss
The Daily News

The whole world is talking about *The Mona Lisa*, with the search for *The Lost Mona Lisa* well and truly now on. The promised £25 million reward is yet to turn up any promising leads, but this journalist understands the royal family has been inundated with crank calls and, it has to be said, extremely poor attempts at copying Leonardo da Vinci's masterpiece. I mean, just look at these – one is a cat! What's that supposed to be? *The Meowna Lisa*?

The Lost Mona Lisa is fast becoming *The Moaning Lisa,* and we all want this mystery solved.

Do you have any suspicions about the whereabouts of this lost masterpiece? Maybe it's been hanging in your hallway so long it's part of the wallpaper? Perhaps a family rumour, long dismissed as a tall tale, has been passed down to you? Did Great Uncle Charlie use to mutter about the stolen painting in his sleep? Whatever your story, get in touch.

Dear Granny,

I'm starting to think that all teachers must be a bit weird. Our most normal teacher is a new guy called Mr Carpsucker (although Smart-Alec Arthur has, of course, started calling him Mr Thumbsucker). He likes everything "just so" - not just in his classroom but throughout the school. I swear I've seen him cleaning the windows in his classroom (I think he must have brought in his own cleaning equipment and rubber gloves), polishing doorknobs and cleaning out gunk from keyholes. He's the only member of staff to insist I take my beret off in lessons - what a control freak! And my beret gives me terrible hat hair. I'd have thought Mr Carpsucker would at least be sympathetic to

NEVER ↘

that, because when he senses his own hair is a mess (which it NEVER is), a comb appears from his pocket and he spends five minutes smoothing down imaginary stray hairs.

In TUBA NEWS, Miss Tench has said I can join the school orchestra already, even though I've only been playing for less than a week and I now know a grand total of TWO NOTES (which don't even come out properly half the time). But if Miss Tench thinks the orchestra can be improved with the addition of what basically sounds like a wet elephant fart, that is her choice! I was really proud to be invited to join the orchestra so soon, but then it turned out even Jake has joined. On the KAZOO! Is that even an instrument? Why can't Jake let me do something on my own?

Maybe, like everyone else, Jake is terrified of Miss Tench. She wears her hair scraped back in a really severe bun and then has bright red lipstick that matches her bright red glasses frames. She's really tiny, but wears these vertigo-inducing stilettos, which click along when she walks up the corridor as if she's her own percussion section. I like her, though. She's said I can keep the tuba at school and practise at lunchtimes because Mum's worried the tuba noise is stressing SEABERT out. She's convinced his skin has lost some of its award-winning purple hue.

At orchestra, I got to speak to Shanice a bit. Turns out the beloved town optician, Mr Michael Chimaera, is *her grandfather*. Like EVERYONE at school, she knows about the whole glasses-stamping episode (no thanks to the very *distinctive* glasses you sent, which continue to remind everyone about it), so I guess that friendship is not going to happen!

Love, Mia

To: Codename Boss Eye

22 High Street, Colpepper

Since taking up my position at Colpepper Hall
School, despite a thorough search of the premises,
I have made no progress in my allotted task, I am
ashamed to report. There is absolutely no sign
anywhere of the five "skeleton keys".
　　The only keys I can spot are the school keys
Mr Scales keeps on his person at all times. If
the skeleton keys were part of that bunch, would
it not follow that the crypt you seek would have
been discovered long ago? The fact that the crypt
and *The Lost Mona Lisa* remain undiscovered makes
me think we need to look at this mystery another
way. Is it possible that I should be looking for
other items that *act* as keys?
　　Please advise.

Your humble lackey,

Codename Iris

From the desk of

Michael Chimaera MP

MC Glasses

22 High Street, Colpepper

To Codename Iris,

Your secret work is just that: SECRET. So don't be contacting me willy-nilly with every last query and concern. I thought I could trust you to handle this.

According to the information passed down to me through the family, skeleton keys access the crypt – that's all I can remember from Lord Colpepper's dog-eared note. If only I hadn't misplaced it! I'm certain the painting is still where he hid it, so keep looking – but be discreet! It goes without saying that the painting **_cannot_** be known to have been found in Colpepper Hall. If that were to happen, people would quickly work out that Lord Colpepper actually stole the painting from his royal friend in the first place – so there's no way a relative of Lord C would be able to claim the reward.

There must be some way of finding out what these

blasted skeleton keys are. Use your imagination for the next steps — but keep my name out of this. I'm a respected member of this community and cannot be linked to anything dodgy, especially since I'm going to "miraculously" discover the lost painting somewhere else.

~~Michael~~ Codename Boss Eye

Dearest Mia,

It's so wonderful to hear about you playing an instrument. And the tuba? What a choice! People always need a tuba in their band. You see, you DO like standing out from the crowd. I used to play percussion instruments, did you know? I was rather an expert on the guiro!

I do like how, in each email, you manage to mention Jake. Perhaps you miss him more than you realize, which is understandable as you've been friends for such a long time. I remember you telling me about performing together in your year six staging of *Oliver!* last year – and how he made such a great Artful Dodger when you played Fagin. You've always had so much fun together. So he got you into trouble with the local optician – so what? Isn't it best just to laugh about that now? I've always had a soft spot for Jake and his dogged determination to uncover the truth, even if he doesn't always get it right – it's that kind of curiosity that led me into journalism. Isn't it time you simply shared a Wagon Wheel and put *the incident* behind you? I'm sure Michael Chimaera has put it behind him. Do you know,

Michael Chimaera was the biggest bully when we were at school? He tried to convince everyone that he was related to Lord Colpepper because he looked a bit like the statue – you see, pompous! He walked round the school like he owned the place and referred to anyone he felt was beneath him as a "minnow", which was basically everybody. Disgusted by his attitude, I was. Mary Mudskipper, the most talented artist in our year, was the main target of Michael's unpleasantness – he used to call her a "bottom feeder" and made her sit on the cold wooden floors.

Perhaps I should thank Michael Chimaera as it was his horridness that prompted me to get far away from Colpepper and, now, here I am, reporting on important scientific research, travelling the world and meeting lots of interesting people. My latest article reports on the challenges of keeping lions from starvation: *Hungry Lions Given a Hand*. Very thought-provoking.

I hope Shanice isn't like her grandfather. If you're meant to be friends, it will happen.

Just about to get my hair done. I fancy a change, so dark blue and curly, I'm thinking! XXX

Kat B. | Freelance journalist for science and nature | fjsn.net
Sent from my phone

EYE FOR TRUTH

by Jake Janowski

Welcome back, fellow truth-seekers!

For this, my second blog, I'm excited to share with you my new discoveries...

I've been watching our head, Mr Scales, and I am SURE he is up to something. Something weird. Something NOT HUMAN. Maybe there's more *reptilian* aspects to Mr Scales than just his creepy lizard eyes. He scuttles around the place, always appearing as if by magic. In an old building like this, I'd wager there's lots of hidden passages and secret doors. Maybe the big bunch of keys he has with him lets him move around unseen.

But *he* can definitely see *us*: there's this weird tannoy system at school, which I think has been in place since Lord Colpepper's time. If someone does something they shouldn't, Mr Scales's voice suddenly hisses out, "Stop running in the corridor, Louise Callaghan," or "Chase McGann! Look at your own work!" I have no idea how he sees all of this! He has eyes EVERYWHERE.

Maybe he's in cahoots with a certain local optician?

But Mr Scales isn't the only thing worth investigating at

school. Take, for instance, the school motto: "Success is at our fingertips." It's a great slogan for a school: encouraging, positive, aspirational. But why are those words carved into the plinth of Lord Colpepper's bust, which was created *long before the building was a school?* Those words must have meant something to Lord Colpepper – but what? And don't even get me started on the school logo, with the weird hand (and it's not a starfish, whatever a *certain person* thinks). Is it the hand of Lord Colpepper, even though he's been dead for around one-hundred-and-eighty years, controlling things?

And now for an update on my research into The Fish. I've got to tell you, finding out The Fish's identity might be trickier than I first imagined. How's this for weird? Try as I might, I haven't been able to find ANY reports about The Fish in the last decade. Did The Fish just disappear off the face of the earth? Did The Fish stop performing heists? You may wonder why I care about some cat burglar from years ago, but The Fish was no ordinary art thief. They were (and probably still are) an artist in their own right. Let me enlighten you:

- Not only were they expert at stealing paintings from under the noses of galleries, they replaced the stolen paintings with a copy that was so exact no one could tell the difference – until the telltale tiny fish was spotted, which The Fish always included in their fake paintings.

- The Fish's plots were always convoluted and complex. You must have heard of the theft of Van Gogh's *Starry Night*? It is suspected The Fish actually worked at the Museum of Modern Art for months as four different members of staff before carrying out their planned heist, which must have taken months, if not years, of planning. Although The Fish worked alone, other people were brought in, generally unwittingly, to act as decoys and stooges, allowing The Fish to escape with the booty.

- The Fish never benefited financially from the stolen paintings and would return them to their rightful owners at some point – so why would The Fish go to these lengths? As a talented artist themselves, why spend a lifetime copying and stealing other people's art?

I would love to have some of these questions answered.

Even though there have been no reports about The Fish for years, I'm certain that if I look hard enough the evidence will be there. I'm on the hunt for any strange goings-on in galleries. Any suspicious activity, I'll log it and create my own dossier of proof. Hopefully, that way, I can find out The Fish's identity.

Number of views: 135   **Likes: 24**

INTERNATIONAL ESPIONAGE AGENCY

SURVEILLANCE REPORT

KEYWORD MONITORING ALERT

Keyword identified: The Fish

Alert level: Low

Action required: None

Hey M,

I keep seeing you talking to Mr Scales. Keep out of his way, unless you want to become lizard food! There's definitely something reptilian about him.

What about this Saturday?

JJ

Dear Granny,

I've already managed to annoy Mr Scales so he thinks I'm this right troublemaker. (OK, so that's not great, but it's for a good cause, right?) All I've done is ask if there is anything I can do about the art department – whenever I see him, which has been, like, ten times a day. Thanks to the magnifying lenses in his glasses, it's become really obvious that his eyes have started to narrow whenever he sees me. He SAYS he's working on a plan to deal with the building and hopefully stop it becoming a car park, but he also said, "What the government decides about funding for art education is out of my hands." Poor Mr Scales. He really does seem very stressed. His skin is starting to look really dry and scaly (ha – like his name) and, as any STARFISH expert will tell you, that's a sure sign of something not being right. ARGH! Why do I know that?

Anyway, probably just to shut me up, Mr Scales has announced an art competition for the school. FANTASTIC! Any picture, any material, any size. It doesn't quite make up for having no art department, teachers or equipment, but it's something, at least – and Mum and Dad can't complain

48

about me working on my entry because it technically counts as schoolwork. Yay! Oooooh, I wonder if Mr Scales will give out a rosette? Wouldn't it be wonderful for SEABERT not to be the only prize-winner in the family? The deadline is Monday 17 October, so I've got less than a month to create my masterpiece.

We got to do our first dissection in biology today. Arthur fainted (ha! Not such a clever clogs then!), which the teacher said is quite normal in his classes, although he's never known a pupil faint at dissecting an onion skin before. The class really laughed at that, but I think maybe Arthur was looking at the VERY graphic drawing of a skeleton hanging on the wall in an old frame, which is all kinds of disgusting. The skin has all been pinned back and the bones are drawn in loads of detail. Secretly, I think it's quite beautiful because it's so well drawn - but if you're a bit squeamish, then I can imagine it would make your stomach turn, especially the left hand, which is quite mangled and missing the little finger.

I'm not sure biology will really be my thing, but I'm enjoying history, even if Mr Carpsucker is SUPER controlling! He's given us a new project to work on, all about the history of Colpepper Hall. But, Mr Carpsucker being Mr Carpsucker, he couldn't just let us *choose* what we were going to study: he has allocated us all different parts of the building and its history to look into. Actually, I'm not complaining at all because I was given Lord Colpepper's paintings to research for my project. I'd like to think my arty outfit is to thank for that!

Now I've got TWO arty things going on. Things are definitely looking up!

And I feel super lucky because other people in class were given things like "windows and doors" and "people who worked at Colpepper Hall". Someone is studying ex-pupils from the school - I wonder if they'll be able to find out something about Mum and Dad, or even you and your friends! Whatever happened to Mary Mudskipper? Any topic is probably better than Arthur Penty's. He has to research the toilets, which I suspect is revenge for the whole "thumbsucker" name-calling. I saw Jake looking disappointed at his allocated "floors of Colpepper Hall" project - I'm guessing Jake would have rather done his project on "Colpepper Hall was built out of an alien spaceship" or something like that!

Jake's now started wearing a school cap, which is fine and allowed and everything, but I can SEE foil tucked underneath it, which is NOT OK. I would ask him about it, but then he'd think we were friends again. AND WE ARE NOT. And don't you be thinking me mentioning him here is any kind of sign that I miss him. Because I do not. Not even a teeny little bit.

TIN FOIL!

But I do wonder if I could have maybe stopped him from becoming like this. What started out as us giggling over the loopy letters people sent into Jake's parents' newspaper has become more like an obsession. We couldn't believe the outrageous conspiracies that people could come up with. Relatives being replaced by clones? Dinosaur aliens taking human form? Bigfoot alive and well and shopping in Asda? But now Jake seems to have become exactly like those people. Maybe if I hadn't agreed to go along with the protest about MC Glasses, I could have put a stop to this weird behaviour before it started?

Speaking of which, Shanice gave me a little wave in orchestra this week, so maybe she doesn't mind so much about the whole mind-control specs thing with her granddad. I am a bit worried about her, though, as she always seems to be going off to see the nurse about headaches. I've seen the look on Jake's face when she does this. Give it a rest, Jake – sometimes people just get headaches!

In TUBA NEWS, we're playing the "Theme from *The Pink Panther*" in orchestra. I always thought that was a cartoon about, well, a pink panther – but turns out it's a film about the theft of a famous jewel called the "Pink Panther". Who knew! I just wish I could practise more at home – not that there's time this weekend as we're driving SEABERT to Sheffield Sea Parks for the September Sheffield Starfish Symposium, where Seabert will have his usual "starring" (ha!) role. If only Seabert wasn't the world's most famous *Pisaster ochraceus*, maybe my parents would have more time for me.

SIGH

And I'm not sure I can spend hours in a car with Mum and Dad hardly talking to each other. It wouldn't be so bad, but we can only drive at twenty-five miles per hour so that Seabert

STARFISH ON BOARD

doesn't get sloshed around too much and arrives at the symposium looking his purpley best. If he gets stressed out, according to Mum, it would be a PISASTER DISASTER!

At least I can be spending the time thinking about what to do for the art competition during the lonnnngggggggggg, slooooooooooowwwwwwww journey.

Love, Mia

Dearest Mia,

Writing quickly now as I've just finished an article on NASA's latest study: ***Astronauts Get to the Bottom of Gas in Space.*** Deadline met, I'm about to take part in a water-skiing competition. You know me – always busy doing things!

It's so splendid that you are passionate about art, it really is. I can't wait to hear what you've planned for the art competition. What a shame Mr Scales is just getting annoyed at your offers of help for the art department, though. I wonder if there's something you can do without him? Are there other people you can get onside? When I was at school, my friend Graham Grunion was really concerned about the bad school dinners, so he put together a petition for the students to sign – and managed to persuade the head to change the menu.

How was the Starfish Symposium? It may be frustrating, but it's probably a good sign that your parents still attend these things ***together*** – maybe there is hope for their relationship. They've always shared a love of aquariums (remember, they had their first-ever date at Colpepper Aquarium) and Seabert was a wedding present from your dad to your mum, so he is a symbol of their love.

I like the sound of your history project – what a great way to learn more about the school and its building. Mary Mudskipper went on to be a great but unappreciated artist, but that's all I can tell you, I'm afraid. And she did somehow manage to put a stop to Michael Chimaera lording it over everyone and going on about his future fortunes, which was a relief for all of us!

Right, better go get ready. XXX

Kat B. | Freelance journalist for science and nature | fjsn.net
Sent from my phone

Dear Granny,

That's a great idea! What an amazing suggestion! That is TOTALLY something I can do.

I'm going to start a PETITION to get signatures to stop the government cutting arts education in schools. YES!

I tried to catch Mr Scales about it but he now seems to just run away whenever he sees me, so I didn't get anywhere about my PETITION with him. But Mr Rothering has actually turned out to be quite helpful and got me set up with my PETITION online. He's happy that I'm taking an interest in important issues and announced to the rest of my tutor group that they could all learn something from my example about being engaged and socially conscious or whatever. I hate it when teachers do something like that. They *think* they're being nice, but actually it just makes you look like a wally. At least Shanice was nodding approvingly.

My entry for the art competition at school is going really well. I've decided to paint a copy of *The MONA LiSA* for it – good, eh? I found a good quality image of it online so am able to copy it, stroke for stroke, on to my own canvas. OK, so the original painting is on a wooden board, but hopefully school won't hold it against me and, other than that, I'm basically becoming Leonardo da Vinci! *Finally*, I'm getting flecks of paint on my smock so I look even more like a proper artist.

To help us with our history projects, Mr Carpsucker allowed us access to some "archives" in the school library, which are like old letters, receipts and other bits of paper. He said we're doing the same kind of work that *actual* historians do, by looking at original source material. He put on some white gloves and used tweezers to lay out different documents, which I thought was him just being careful with historic documents, but then he also used these same things to give us our exercise books, so I think he just *really* doesn't like dirt.

From what I could find out, Lord Colpepper seemed to be more interested in displaying stuffed animals than paintings. Why would anyone want to stuff a lion and display it in their living room? Yucky! Although, maybe his taste in paintings wasn't much better, as it turns out that Lord Colpepper only had five paintings in his ENTIRE art collection, all of which hung in the Dome Area! Even if there's only five of them, I'm finding this project really fascinating. What makes someone decide to buy a picture? And how do they decide where to put it? If you're Mum, you only buy diagrams of aquatic creatures to display EVERYWHERE, and the reason you do this is that you are starfish obsessed (and thanks for the history lesson in your email but I get the whole " SEABERT was our first child" story from Mum very regularly, so I don't need a reminder!) - but for *normal* people, there are probably more interesting reasons.

I'd love to see Lord Colpepper's five paintings. Just doing this project has made me realize how many great artists and paintings there are that I have no idea about – and not all paintings appear online or in books. If Lord Colpepper's paintings were sea-creature-themed, I'd stand a chance of persuading Mum and Dad to take me to see them, but they're highly unlikely to agree to take me to one gallery, let alone the FIVE different galleries where Lord Colpepper's paintings now hang.

Shanice was allocated a project about the different people who worked at Colpepper Hall. Apparently her granddad is always going on about how he's related to Lord C and what an amazing person he was, and how he did loads for the local area – but Shanice's research about the servants is making her wonder whether Lord Colpepper was NOT such an amazing person after all. She's seriously hoping that her granddad is wrong about being related to Lord Colpepper, because if *he's* related to him, that means she is too!

Meanwhile, Jake hasn't tried to talk or write to me AT ALL for several days – thank goodness for that. (You're not ALWAYS right, you know). He's really taken his project to heart, constantly staring down at the ground. I guess the floors of Colpepper Hall are more interesting than I could have imagined? I'm almost tempted to ask him about it ... almost, but not quite.

Love, Mia

Exclusive!

Call off the search: *The Lost Mona Lisa* has been found!

By Gerta Lowdaviss
The Daily News

This newspaper can exclusively reveal that a Mr H. Oaksy has found the long-lost painting in an ancient cowshed in rural Wiltshire. The missing masterpiece was found, frameless and covered in dung, with only the famous smile peeking out from under the manure. The work has been sealed in an airtight container and is being taken, under armed guard, to Buckingham Palace, where it will be verified.

More information to follow.

View comments

Related Topics

| Art | Royal Family | Mona Lisa | Culture |

To Codename Iris,

How can this be? MY painting, found in some random shed in Wiltshire? I knew my ancestor had a reputation as a lying cad but I was convinced Lord Colpepper was being truthful about the location of *that which you seek*.

I guess that's it, then. Years of plotting and planning for nothing. It's over.

Codename Boss Eye

EYE FOR TRUTH

by Jake Janowski

Back for more, I see, loyal truth-seekers.

Ready to be enlightened?

Well, let me start with something that's been bothering me this week – and maybe, if you're local to Colpepper, it's been bothering you too? Am I the only person who's noticed the weird noise at school? Not the high-pitched noises that have been giving other people headaches – no, not those, I mean a weird chirruping sound.

Anyone?

I can't help but think it's something to do with Mr Scales. I'm certain he knows I'm on to him. I haven't seen him sunning himself on the roof of the east wing for a few days now – although, it is getting colder out there, so... What I *have* seen is several large packages being delivered. Large enough for – oh, I don't know – maybe a SUNBED. Because, when you are a LIZARD MAN, you need to get your heat quota somehow, don't you? And where better to stash this than somewhere no one else can go – like a closed-down art department?

I've yet to hear about any children going missing, so it doesn't appear as though Mr Scales has developed a taste for human flesh

– yet. But don't worry about me, my faithful readers, I'm managing to keep under the radar. Mr Scales hasn't shouted out my name once from the weird old tannoy system.

But MAYBE there's a reason for that. MAYBE he wants to lull me into a false sense of security. MAYBE he's just waiting for me to make my move.

For the safety of my fellow schoolmates, I need to find out what is going on. I need to gain access to the east wing – but Mr Scales never lets the set of keys out of his sight.

For now, I am biding my time.

And how's this for a coincidence? **(Not that there are any coincidences, just links that other people are too blind to notice!)** As I studied the floor of Colpepper Hall for what *should* be the MOST POINTLESS PROJECT IN THE HISTORY OF HISTORY PROJECTS, do you know what I noticed carved into the floorboards? Little fish! Tiny, perfect little fish. Some have been worn down over years of pupils traipsing over them, but they're there. They just haven't been noticed, as no one has been looking for them – until now. And they look *very similar* to the fish found painted on The Fish's fake paintings!

Have I found a clue to The Fish's identity? Is it possible that The Fish attended Colpepper Hall School? Now THAT'S something to think about!

INTERNATIONAL ESPIONAGE AGENCY

SURVEILLANCE REPORT

KEYWORD MONITORING ALERT

Keyword identified: The Fish

Alert level: Low

Action required: None

"We Are Not Amused": Royal Family Respond to Hoaxy "Joke"

By Gerta Lowdaviss
The Daily News

The notorious street artist Hoaxy has revealed himself (or herself) to be behind a pretend version of *The Lost Mona Lisa*, which had many people fooled. *The Lost Mona Lisa* remains lost despite excitement over the last few days that it had been found in a cowshed by a Mr H. Oaksy.

Still missing

According to an anonymous palace insider, when the "found" painting was removed from its airtight container, in front of the *most senior* members of the royal family, there was a loud click and circus music started to play. On contact with the air, the "dung" started to react, giving off a foul-smelling stench. The dung then started liquefying and sliding off the canvas, taking the top layer of paint with it. According to our source, the royal family were left staring at a painting of three clowns, pointing out of the canvas and laughing. A statement issued by the ever-camera-shy Hoaxy read as follows:

"It is heartbreaking to see that money can be made readily

available for the return of an already very famous painting – but where is the financial support for struggling artists and galleries? Where is the financial support for talented youngsters? The media circus surrounding the hunt for *The Lost Mona Lisa* would be better served highlighting the wonderful contemporary artists that are working right now. No one can deny the genius of Leonardo da Vinci, but how will future da Vincis ever be produced without the proper support?"

A spokesperson from the palace criticized Hoaxy's joke as a "stunt" and dismissed Hoaxy's statement as "attention-seeking and self-aggrandizing".

View comments

Related Topics

| Art | Royal Family | Mona Lisa | Culture |

From the desk of

Michael Chimaera MP

MC Glasses

22 High Street, Colpepper

To Codename Iris,

Oh, thank goodness. Panic over.

As you were.

Codename Boss Eye

Dearest Mia,

I'm so delighted to hear about your petition. I've been sure to tell all my friends. I think lots of people will be happy to sign it. Did you know, you can get your local MP to take it to parliament? 100,000 signatures for it to be debated, I believe. I'm sure you could find 100,000 people to sign. Surely we're not the only ones who think arts education is worth saving?

Knowing how talented you are (and not just because you take after me), I'm sure you'll do a wonderful job of copying *The Mona Lisa* for the art competition – but is that the best thing to do? There is definitely a use to copying great works of art but, really, art should be an expression of the artist's own thoughts and feelings. What are you expressing by copying *The Mona Lisa*? I think you're right that you need to start visiting galleries to learn more about your taste in art. Maybe your project on Lord Colpepper's paintings is just the opportunity you needed. I know you think there's no hope, but why not ask your parents about visiting the galleries? It's surely worth a try?

Best sign off. Nina Nase is teaching me how to steer a gondola shortly and I haven't quite finished my latest article: *City Baffled by Stinky Sewer.* XXX

Kat B. | Freelance journalist for science and nature | fjsn.net
Sent from my phone

From: MiaB@StarfishInstructions.net ☰ ✕
To: KBerg55@fjsn.net
Date: 14 October
Subject: Just my luck!

Dear Granny,

Getting my *PETITION* debated in parliament would be incredible! And I'm getting more signatures by the day. It looks like I'm not the only person that thinks studying the arts is important. In tutorial, Arthur said he wasn't interested in signing because he wants to design computer games when he's older, which are just to do with technology, not art – but Mr Rothering pointed out that if Arthur wants his games to look nice, he'll probably need to study some kind of art too – BOOM! Another signature!

Even Mum and Dad have said they're quite impressed with how it's going. I'm now up to 24,987, so the numbers have just EXPLODED. Maybe there's a chance I could get to 100,000 signatures – possibly even by Christmas.

And your suggestion of getting the local Colpepper Member of Parliament involved would have been great, had it not been for

one

   key

      issue:

         Colpepper's MP is Mr Michael Chimaera.

ARGH!

He's not going to help me, is he? Even if I am now a kind-of friend of his granddaughter's!

Why did I have to stamp on those stupid glasses? Who knew that our actions back then would still have consequences now? Grrrrr! It just goes to show I am almost definitely better off *not* being friends with Jake. Aren't I?

I think you're wrong about my painting for the art competition. It's going to be so good, no one will be able to tell the difference between mine and the original. I thought great artists learned by copying old paintings? Didn't you tell me that? Surely, if I copy it really well, I'll win the competition? You'll see!

I know you're eager to receive some TUBA NEWS, so you'll be pleased to hear that I now know eight notes and not one of them sounds like a rhino with diarrhoea (most of the time). Miss Tench is pleased with me in orchestra because she likes that I play loud (although, to be fair, I'm not sure how to play any quieter). We're now learning the theme tunes from the films *A Fish Called Wanda*, *American Hustle* and *The Great Train Robbery*. Miss Tench definitely likes her film tunes!

I'm trying to spend a bit more time with Shanice but she's often busy with her own things. Her bag is covered with badges that say things like "eco-warrior" and I often see her badgering teachers about organizing proper recycling systems in their classrooms or suggesting that writing down work would just be a waste of paper. I see them getting frustrated with her, which I guess is how Mr Scales feels with me bugging him about the art department. The only time she stops is either when she goes off to the school office because of a headache (seriously, how many headaches can someone have?) or when we're at orchestra. She doesn't really seem that bothered about making friends with anyone, so I can't see her as a Jake replacement, but I'd like to get to know her better. I had been thinking about suggesting playing a duet with her as a way to make friends, but who's ever heard of a flute duetting with a TUBA? It'd be a ridiculous suggestion.

Love, *Mia*

Dearest Mia,

I'm a firm believer that everything happens for a reason. You'll see I'm right. Don't worry about getting Michael Chimaera involved. Who needs a silly MP? They just make lots of noise, and I'm sure you can think of a way to do that without him. Yes, having his support would help to get parliament to debate funding for arts education, but I'm sure there are other ways you can do this. With everything being online nowadays, it's too easy for people to sign things, but they forget to go the extra mile – so why not think about what you can do to make your petition stand out? Why not take it down to London yourself? Have you ever been here before? This would be a marvellous opportunity.

I'm briefly in London right now, finishing up my latest article ***Most Significant Factor in Flooding: Rain***. I've just visited the Thames Barrier and am now heading up the river on a boat. It's a wonderful way to see the city, but I fear I've snagged my stockings. Must buy more before I leave for my next destination!

I do like hearing all of your news. Orchestra sounds just wonderful – and what quirky pieces you seem to be playing! That's reminded me – when I played in orchestras in my youth, we used to go around busking in town squares and shopping centres. Made a big noise, we did! XXX

Kat B. | Freelance journalist for science and nature | fjsn.net
Sent from my phone

Dear Granny,

You're so full of good suggestions! **Of course!** I could take my PETITION down to London! And then that gave me an even more GENIUS thought: maybe I could try and get Miss Tench on board so that the WHOLE ORCHESTRA could have a trip to London and maybe even do some busking somewhere to help make money for the school's arts programme!

How's that for a BRILLIANT idea?

Maybe you could help me think of where we could do something like that? I've never been to London before – it would be so awesome!

Everything has been coming to an end this week because of next week's holiday. I handed my entry in for the art competition and my history project this week. And guess what? After I researched all the paintings, I realized that each of the five paintings contains a skeleton! How's that for a discovery, and just before Halloween, too. Mr Carpsucker was so impressed with mine, he gave it an A+++++, which I'm not sure is even a grade, and he called it "enlightening and very useful"!

Shanice got really into her project. You

wouldn't BELIEVE the kinds of things Lord Colpepper used to get up to. Apparently, he was in MASSES of debt because he kept gambling. He was friends with King George IV and they basically just used to party all the time. Shanice even found evidence that Lord Colpepper locked his first wife up and pretended to everyone she was unwell, just so he could divorce her and marry someone else. AND THEN, when his money ran out and he no longer had any servants, Lord Colpepper would send his second wife out disguised as a servant to scrub the OUTSIDE courtyard, just to make sure that local people still thought he was wealthy enough to have servants! Doesn't Lord Colpepper sound awful?

Well, Shanice certainly thinks so - so she's started her *own* petition. She doesn't think that Lord Colpepper should have so many things named after him, so her petition is to try to change the name of the town and our school. She also wants his statue removed from the school's entrance hall. When Shanice was presenting her project, she was just so passionate about it all - it was really impressive. She asked, "Why do we keep paying tribute to people from history who don't deserve the attention?" and made the point that Lord Colpepper never had to work for anything in his life, so he's not exactly a role model for us pupils, which is a very fair point. My signature is the very first one on Shanice's petition.

I think Shanice's project was the best, but Mr Carpsucker only awarded it an A - which seems really unfair as it was at least as good as mine, and she studied loads of people who'd worked at Colpepper Hall; I only had to study five paintings! Jake didn't even hand his project in; apparently he needed more time. For what? It's a project about floors! I wish I knew what Jake is up to. I used to know EVERYTHING he was thinking. I hope he's not getting himself into trouble. The Jake I knew would never have handed in a piece of work late.

Why do we have to wait until AFTER the half-term holiday to find out who won the school's art competition? It's so painful waiting that long, especially when I'm certain to win. My painting was awesome compared to the other entries!

Love, *Mia*

PS Esme, who studied the ex-pupils of Colpepper Hall School, showed lots of photos of classes over the years. I managed to spot Dad and Mum in one, and I think I saw you and Michael Chimaera in another. I asked Esme about your friend, Mary Mudskipper, but she said she didn't see anything about anyone of that name. It's not surprising, really, as there must have been thousands of students over the years.

To Codename Boss Eye

MC Glasses

22 High Street, Colpepper

I have made a breakthrough regarding the *you know what*!

The skeleton keys were not keys at all. I believe that **five pictures** are the KEY to finding the CRYPT. The only five pictures that *you know who* owned just happen to be of SKELETONS – surely that's too much of a coincidence?

And look at this, these are their titles and artists:

- *Time Bowing to Death*
by Cranach the Elder (1472–1553)

- *Study of a Splayed Corpse*
by Rubens (1577–1640)

- *Winter Scene*
by Brueghel the Younger (1564–1637)

- *Landscape with Death*
by Poussin (1594–1665)

- *Sketch of a Broken Skeleton* (left hand)
by Turner (1775–1851)

And not only do these paintings contain skeletons — surely making them *what we seek* — check out this extra-genius discovery by YOURS TRULY: the first letters of the surnames of the artists spell out CRYPT! Just what we're looking for! This is surely the biggest clue that these paintings are, indeed, the key to locating the crypt. I know, in your pedantic and perfectionist way, you're going to point out that Brueghel the Younger actually starts with a B, not a Y, but I guess artists with surnames beginning with Y were pretty hard to come by.

Having studied all I can about these five paintings since making my genius discovery — there is disappointingly little about the five paintings published online — I am increasingly convinced that the only way to decipher any meaning left to us by Lord Colpepper is to bring the paintings back together in their original locations in the school's Dome Area. Once there, I am sure the answer will reveal itself. I'm certain they'll lead us to *what we seek*.

Unfortunately, however, the five paintings are in five different galleries and we can't just walk in and ask to borrow them.

Just how am I supposed to get hold of these

paintings? It's not like I'm an expert art thief.
And you know I don't like getting my hands dirty.
What should I do?

From

Codename Iris

HISTORY PROJECT

BY

JAKE JANOWKSI

"THE FLOORS OF COLPEPPER HALL SCHOOL"

or

"A DAZZLING EXPOSÉ OF AN NOTORIOUS ART THIEF'S IDENTITY" — goodness!

TOP SECRET

FOR MR CARPSUCKER'S EYES ONLY

— Quite right. Don't want
this information falling into
the wrong hands!

When you gave me this project, sir, I thought it was going to be (dead boring) because what's interesting about flooring? How wrong I was! — too informal

At first, I thought the only interesting bit of flooring in Colpepper Hall School was probably the weird spindly hand pattern on the floor of the Dome Area - you know, that mosaic floor around the bust of Lord Colpepper? I bet I'm the only pupil in the history of the school to notice that the spindly hand on the floor matches the weird hand on the school logo! Do you know that there are gaps in the floor between the grey tiles of the fingers and the white tiles of the rest of the floor? I don't mean just a bit of grouting missing - I slid whole pieces of paper down there. Lots of them. Where were they going? I didn't have time to look into this more, and I know this was *supposed* to be a project on the floors of Colpepper Hall, but, I hope you'll agree, what I've discovered is FAR MORE INTERESTING:

I found carvings of little fish and, based on research I'd been carrying out anyway, I am fairly certain these link to the notorious art thief, The Fish. Not only that, but these carvings have given me a clue to The Fish's identity - something that no authorities have been able to work out! The carvings tell me that The Fish must have, at some time, been a pupil at (Codpepper) Hall School, so I started to think about who it could be. — Sp

While considering this, I happened to spot the entries for

the school's art competition and one in particular caught my eye - a painting that is so good, the famous enigmatic smile has been captured perfectly. A picture so good, it could have been painted by Leonardo da Vinci himself. A picture SO GOOD, it could be confused for *The Lost Mona Lisa*, were it not for the signature of Mia Berghler in the bottom right-hand corner. And that's when the penny dropped - Mia is a talented artist because she's related to talented artists - isn't that how these things work?

I believe I've cracked it:

- Who was a pupil at Colpepper Hall School?
- Who has expertize in alarms and electronic equipment?
- Who is suspiciously UNINTERESTED in any kind of art?
- Who LOVES aquatic creatures and is completely besotted with their pet starfish?
- Who is always travelling around the country under the guise of attending fish festivals?

If you read between the lines, you can come up with only one conclusion:

Lovely. Building suspense through asking questions.

My best friend's parents are **THE FISH**.

Oh yes, no wonder THE FISH has never been identified before. No *one* person could plan such great art heists AND copy paintings so perfectly. It *had* to be a team. And the word FISH can mean **ONE** fish or it can mean **MANY** fish. You see? *Well spotted*

And finally, I'd like to bring your attention to the email

address of their business: StarfishInstructions.Net

What does this name spell out when rearranged? **ART HEISTS**, that's what (plus a few other letters, but they're surely not relevant). This, I think you will agree, proves my point without any shadow of a doubt. ←

In conclusion, floors are actually quite interesting and The Fish is Mr and Mrs Berghler (but keep that last bit to yourself, because I don't want my best friends parents to get into trouble).

apostrophe needed

Fear not. Your secret is safe with me.

That is called anagram. Grea build up yo word pow

To Codename Boss Eye

MC Glasses

22 High Street, Colpepper

Ignore the last message. A solution has presented
itself.

Codename Iris

Hey M,

Sorry if I've been ignoring you lately. All OK with you?
Anything FISHY you want to tell me about?
Remember I'm here for you.
Any plans for half-term? We have a huge stash of
Wagon Wheels so come over whenever.

JJ

J,

What are you going on about?

Are you that desperate for new conspiracy theories that you're now asking me to come up with them for you? **SOMETHING FISHY, INDEED!**

All the Wagon Wheels in the world wouldn't make me come to yours.

And, besides, I'm busy.

M

From: MiaB@StarfishInstructions.net ≡ ×
To: KBerg55@fjsn.net
Date: 22 October
Subject: Half-term hell

Dear Granny,

These first weeks of secondary school have been EXHAUSTING, but I wish I could say I'm glad to be on holiday. I would LOVE to be able to spend a week in bed, *but* Mum and Dad have drawn up a schedule which includes spending a whole day today cleaning Seabert's travel tank and then taking a VERY SLOW drive up to Newcastle for the *Half-term Hoedown of Scary Sea Creatures and Creepy Crustaceans*. We go every year and I'm sick of it. Why do we all have to dress up as starfish? And MY starfish costume was made when I was nine before my growth spurt. I'm torn between mentioning this and having to spend a day papier-mâchéing a new costume with Mum or just putting up with the old one and the danger of flashing my bum at everyone. It's a dilemma!

I've been whingeing and fussing so much about having to go to this stupid Half-term Hoedown AGAIN that I have managed to persuade them – on the LAST day of the holiday – to spend the day with me in Colpepper, getting more people to sign my **PETITION**. I may have employed emotional blackmail but this could be the *first-ever time* that Mum and

Dad have done something just for me, so I'm accepting it! TOTALLY WORTH IT! It was actually Mr Carpsucker who suggested it when I was talking to him about my half- term and complaining to him about SEABERT. He was genuinely interested and supportive about my PETITION, and so sympathetic to my feelings about SEABERT. I think he liked my history project so much that he can see why it is important for me to still be able to study art. Do you know, like you, he even suggested that I try to get Mum and Dad to take me to see the five pictures from Lord Colpepper's collection in the five galleries? Ha! As if *that* will ever happen. But getting Mum and Dad out and about in town to drum up more signatures for my petition is a start, so that's something.

Love, Mia

EYE FOR TRUTH

by Jake Janowski

Faithful followers, your loyalty is about to be rewarded!

You may be reading this in the hope of more information about the Lizard Leader, Mr Scales, but this week's blog is exposing something EVEN MORE INCREDIBLE.

I have done it! I have succeeded in my mission to discover the true identity of The Fish.

HOWEVER, for the safety of The Fish and their loved ones, I have taken the very hard decision not to share this information with my public. If I put anyone in danger, I wouldn't be able to live with myself. But I will say this – I do believe that reports on The Fish and their actions over the last ten years have been quashed and suppressed by the authorities. *"Why would anyone do this?"* I hear you cry. Well, let me tell you:

Why do people go to art galleries to see art?

Nowadays, we can see very easily any painting we want on the internet with a push of a button. Paintings are reproduced endlessly on T-shirts, glasses cases, magnets, postcards.

The only reason to go to a gallery is to see THE ORIGINAL painting – and people really value knowing they're seeing the one

true version, touched by the hand of a **genius artist**.

BUT WHAT IF galleries could not guarantee to their visitors that their displayed paintings were the real deal? _**People would**_ _**stop visiting.**_ And that's what was happening when news outlets were reporting on The Fish's activities years ago – it made people stop visiting galleries. So, somewhere in the corridors of power, I think the decision was taken to stop reporting The Fish's activities. It still goes on, but WE don't hear about it because someone doesn't WANT us to hear about it. And we happily carry on in blissful ignorance. No wonder the dossier I wanted to create was proving really difficult to put together! I wonder how many of The Fish's fake paintings are hanging in galleries around the world right now. Get out there and check, my truth-seekers!

Number of views: 7,925   **Likes:** 1,652

INTERNATIONAL ESPIONAGE AGENCY

SURVEILLANCE REPORT

KEYWORD MONITORING ALERT

Keyword identified: The Fish

Alert level: High

Action required: Query

For the attention of
Sir Mustard-Greens, Head of the
International Espionage Agency

Dear Sir,

I know we are not supposed to report on The Fish
or any activities around them, but our keyword
monitoring system keeps flagging use of the term
"The Fish" on a public blog. Not only that, the
blogger (an eleven-year-old schoolboy) is now
claiming that he knows the identity of The Fish.
Having failed to identify The Fish for years, a child
has apparently done the work for us. Unfortunately
for our intelligence services, he hasn't named the
person he suspects.

Not only that. The blogger has claimed that the
authorities have been failing to report on The
Fish's activities for years, intentionally quashing
stories so that people will continue to visit art
galleries - and he's starting to build quite a
following. Can we risk him continuing to spread his
theories when he's just hit the nail on the head?

He might be some confused conspiracy theorist

- you should see what he's been writing about his headmaster - but he's spot-on with this. What shall we do? Please advise.

Yours faithfully,

Agent Carrot

From Sir Mustard-Greens,
Head of IEA

Agent Carrot,

Top-notch surveillance, my good chap. The official position remains unchanged: no reporting on The Fish. However, I can see that this blog nonsense is putting us in a bit of a pickle. As far as I can see, no one should take this child's theories seriously - lizard men? Mind-control specs? However, he is right about the reporting of The Fish's activities being suppressed and so maybe he has actually worked out the true identity of The Fish. It would be jolly useful if he has, as that dastardly Fish has been making fools of all of us for too many years to count! Sadly, there's no money in the budget for putting extra agents on this, but, as we're talking about a schoolchild here, let's pop one of our new Wildgoose Academy recruits into Colpepper Hall School to see what they can find out. Should be a straightforward intelligence-gathering operation, don't you agree?

Carry on.

Sir M-G

Art Galleries Report Bumper Visitor Numbers

By Gerta Lowdaviss
The Daily News

Art galleries across the country are reporting unusually high visitor figures since the announcement of the £25 million reward for *The Lost Mona Lisa*. Dubbed *"The Lost Mona Lisa Lift"*, the figures show that members of the public have embraced the search for the famous painting, and the publicity around the hunt has encouraged

Still lost

more people to appreciate art. Well, either that or people are going to galleries in the hope that they will spot the world's most famous missing painting just hanging in the corner of a public institution, which hardly seems credible, in this journalist's opinion!

View comments

Related Topics

| Art | Royal Family | Mona Lisa | Culture |

To Codename Pupil

Ready your team. Codename Iris has gone rogue – first contacting me asking about art thieves and then saying that he's sorting it. What is he up to? I should have known better than to trust him. I worry he's going to ruin my chance of claiming the reward. Thankfully, whatever he is planning, he is unaware that I DO have a crack team of cat burglars up my sleeve.

Infiltrate the school, observe and await my instructions.

And, as always, you don't know me and your work has nothing to do with me.

From

Codename Boss Eye

Dear Granny,

We got back from gathering signatures in the centre of Colpepper about two hours ago. Mum went in to check on SEABERT and there was this BIG SCREAM. Mum and Dad both disappeared off for ages and now they won't tell me what's going on. But SEABERT is no longer in his tank! Can this be true?

Has he finally kicked the bucket?

Mum and Dad look like they have both been crying. I keep waiting for them to tell me that he's died, but whenever they open their mouths to speak to me, they just start sobbing instead.

I've been imagining this moment for years, and I always thought I would be thrilled ... but you know what? I'm not. I can't be happy about something that makes them this upset. We'd had a really good day collecting signatures, and it was so GREAT to be doing something together as a family that did not involve SEABERT, but now everything's gone horribly wrong. I heard Mum say to Dad, "If only one of us had stayed behind." I hope they're not blaming *me* for Seabert's death, just because they both came to help with my petition!

But am I allowed to be a *little* pleased that SEABERT is gone? Now I won't have to play second fiddle to a starfish! One thing I am glad about is that Mum and Dad at least are hugging and being nice to each other for once.

Love, Mia

RIP
SEABERT
☆

PS I also know it isn't the time to be boasting, but we're now up to 64,978 signatures. Isn't that great?

Mr and Mrs Berghler (if those are your **real**
names),

I know who you are. There is no point trying to
deny it.

I have your starfish. Do as I say and no harm
will come to ~~him it~~ the starfish.

I need five paintings stolen from five different
galleries and I believe you are the people who
can do this.

You will perform five art heists for me.

Each heist successfully done is a starfish
~~tentacle leg~~ arm saved. Five heists for five
starfish arm thingies. A fair deal, I'd say.

Tell no one.

I will be in touch.

Dear Granny,

I'm gutted.

I didn't win.

How can that be?

I'M the artist of the school – anyone looking at my beret and smock can see that!

The winner was announced in assembly this morning, which started off bad enough when Mr Scales said he had an exciting announcement about a donation. I jumped up, ready to celebrate, thinking he must have got some money to save the art department, but NO. Turns out an anonymous donor has come forward to help pay for some extra staff – so we now have some new dinner people, a caretaker and a school nurse, called Carrie, Barry, Larry and Harry (but not necessarily in that order). Big whoop. So there's still no good news about the art department.

Then Mr Scales said he was going to announce the art competition winner. I was so confident it was me, I jumped up just before the name was said (I should really wait till I hear the end of announcements before jumping up) - but it wasn't me, the winner was Shanice! SO UNFAIR! *She* hadn't precisely copied a world-famous masterpiece. Hers was just lots of different blobs of green, turning to blobs of black, titled *The Earth: The Future*. Mr Scales went on about it being really *expressive*, *relevant* and *personal* as he presented her with a big rosette. Whatever. What does *he* know about art?

To make things worse, Jake has gone back to trying to tell me the WEIRD IDEAS that he's got in his head. Like today, when we were waiting to get lunch, he kept trying to get my attention and was holding up the queue - much to the annoyance of the new boy in our year, Garry. I wasn't going to give him the satisfaction, but I could see him out the corner of my eye, pointing at the new dinner men, Barry and Larry. I have no idea what he was *trying* to tell me, but those men are so massive and hulking, I wouldn't want to get on their wrong side. I hope Jake doesn't have a weird theory about them.

Barry (or was it Larry?) did seem to give Jake quite a GLARE as he slopped pink custard over his sponge, but maybe he glares at everyone. I'm concerned that

Jake's weird theories, which were always just a bit of a laugh, have started to get more far-fetched. Not that Jake's my responsibility, but I don't want to see him dunked in a vat of pink custard for annoying the serving staff.

Mum and Dad are still in a complete state over SEABERT. Dad is in full-on blanky-cuddling mode. But they STILL haven't actually told me he is dead. In fact, they keep giving all kinds of different reasons for why he's gone. Mum even tried telling me he's gone for a special spa treatment, while Dad said he was off getting fitted for a new tank. They might as well try to tell me he's gone to that *special farm* that takes all the sick dogs and cats - I'm not seven!

Or maybe THEY aren't ready to accept that Seabert has gone. I guess Mum and Dad are grieving over Seabert. I've been reading up about grief and apparently there are five stages to it. The first stage is DENIAL. No wonder they haven't been able to bring themselves to tell me.

Love, *Mia*

Hey M,

I think your painting was **THE BEST**. But maybe don't show your talent too obviously so no one else works out the truth. Don't worry - your family secret is safe with me.

JJ

PS watch out for The Clones!

EYE FOR TRUTH

by Jake Janowski

Welcome back, faithful readers.

I know, I know, I see in the comments that you are dying to find out who The Fish is, but I'm keeping that secret to myself ... for now. I don't want to hurt anyone by revealing the truth.

But don't you worry! There are more unsettling mysteries here in Colpepper left to be uncovered! In fact, I can report on a dramatic new development:

I thought that having a monstrous lizard man for a headmaster was bad. But something *even worse* may be going on! I think the school might be being targeted by CLONES! Has anyone else noticed that the four new members of staff, anonymously "donated" to the school, all look identical – all big and hulking, looming over the students? Well, I *think* there's only four of them. Maybe that's just what they want us to think. Maybe there's twenty of them, or forty! The only pupil they don't seem to loom over is the new year seven, Garry. But I ask you: could he be ONE OF THEM? Please don't tell me I'm the only one who's seen this? Why is everyone else so BLIND to these weird goings-on?

Whoever they are, I want to know what they are doing at our

school. Are they part of Mr Scales's lizard plans? To be fair, they don't look much like lizards, with their potato faces and great hulking bodies. Or maybe I am getting too close to the truth in this blog and they've been sent to silence me? If this *is* my last blog, you'll know why – spread the word, faithful readers!

Number of views: 13,654   **Likes:** 3,422

INTERNATIONAL ESPIONAGE AGENCY

SURVEILLANCE REPORT

KEYWORD MONITORING ALERT

Keyword identified: The Fish

Alert level: N/A

Action required: Operative assigned

From: KBerg55@fjsn.net

To: MiaB@StarfishInstructions.net

Date: 1 November

Subject: Hallo from Belgium

Dearest Mia,

Your poor parents – they must be very sad. Try to be sympathetic, won't you? You know, when my friend Paula Parore's pet parrot, Petunia, died, the thing that helped her most was going back to places she'd taken Petunia. Perhaps this might help your parents too? And, you never know – if you do something nice for them, maybe it will benefit you too. Are you still wanting to see those paintings by Lord Colpepper? Maybe you can suggest a visit where you'd all get to do things you like?

And I'm so sorry to hear about the art competition. I know you're upset now, but don't be disheartened. Remember, it takes more than an outfit and copying paintings to be an artist!

Things will start looking up soon, you'll see. It's easy to feel down when lots of bad things seem to be happening, but perhaps it's all part of a bigger plan. Speaking of which, you've got your trip to London to plan!

Got to go – here in Belgium with my friend, I am. Deborah Dab and

I are about to tuck into a steaming bowl of mussels and chips. (A bit of a treat after scooping an exclusive: *"We Just Don't Like Mice," World's Scientists Finally Admit*). XXX

Kat B. | Freelance journalist for science and nature | fjsn.net
Sent from my phone

Dear Granny,

Oh! My! Goodness!

You won't believe this!

You were right!

I took your advice and suggested going up to Scotland to the Falkirk Fish Festival next weekend, which is something Mum and Dad would normally have attended with SEABERT. They didn't seem that enthusiastic, but when I casually mentioned it would also be an opportunity to see one of the Lord Colpepper paintings at the National Galleries, Scotland, they suddenly seemed to think the trip was a good idea. They really seemed keen to take me – and not just to see the one painting, but to visit ALL FIVE! Mum even said it was "important" for us to go. IMPORTANT! Finally! They're seeing my interest in art as IMPORTANT!

Maybe losing SEABERT has made them lose their minds a bit. I mean, who *are* these people? Not that I'm suggesting my parents have been abducted by aliens and replaced with robots (argh – get out of my head, Jake!).

And bless them – they seem to be taking the visit quite seriously. I think they must be quite nervous, having not been to a gallery for YEARS. They're looking online at the collections and the gallery plan. I just assumed that people walk into galleries off the street all the time, without having to plan their trip in every minute detail, but hey, if it gets us into a gallery, I'm not complaining!

At school, everyone in year seven suddenly had to take an eye test this week. (Well, everyone except Jake, who ran off goodness knows where when he saw Michael Chimaera.) Mr Chimaera looked a little surprised at my glasses (I don't care what anyone thinks of them now – I like them!), but you'll be pleased to hear I could see the chart perfectly – good news for visiting my first-ever gallery. Other children seemed to struggle, like Garry, the new kid. He read the chart over and over, like he was trying to memorize it or something. Poor guy.

Love, Mia

C

O D

E N A

M E I R

I S P L A

N S T O S T

E A L T H E F

I V E P A I N T

I N G S S O M E H

O W F I N D O U T H

O W W H E R E A N D W

H E N F O L L O W A N D

S T E A L I N S T E A D B

R I N G T H E M T O M E M C

J,

It was only an eye test! Forget MC Glasses.
You're becoming paranoid. Even if we no
longer hang out, I don't want you getting
into trouble at school.

M

From: KBerg55@fjsn.net   ☰ ✕

To: MiaB@StarfishInstructions.net

Date: 10 November

Subject: Agoo from Ghana

Dearest Mia,

How wonderful! Just a very quick response to say HAVE FUN ON YOUR FIRST-EVER GALLERY VISIT! I really hope you enjoy the experience. Keep your eyes open and take everything in. I can't wait to hear about it.

Must dash – got to send off my article on the breaking news: *Ghanaian Meteorite May Be From Space*. XXX

Kat B. | Freelance journalist for science and nature | fjsn.net
Sent from my phone

Dear Granny,

I LOVED IT!!!!

Galleries are the best.

Art and talent and inspiration all in one place. AMAZING! Just standing looking at all those works of art, I felt like I was absorbing some of the talent.

And it was FREE, which was fantastic because it means that anyone can go and see the stuff.

Mum and Dad were definitely nervous, but I think they enjoyed it too – they were *really* interested. Dad was busy trying to spot the hidden wires and switches. So typical of Dad – always working! He even got into a REALLY BORING conversation with a security guard about their new Verisafe Alarm 3000. I could hear the security guard boasting that, "We just need to have someone look at our paintings the wrong way and sirens blare out like England have won the World Cup." Good to know – I'll make sure I keep my hands to myself – ha ha!

Even Mum and Dad stopped to have a proper look at *Time Bowing to Death* – the picture from Lord Colpepper's collection – and they even seemed VAGUELY interested while I told them what I knew about the painting from my project research. The painting is by Cranach the Elder, which is a silly name – he can't always have been old, so why is he called the Elder? It was so thrilling to be within touching distance of a real masterpiece – so much better than just seeing these paintings in books or online. Mum and Dad gave me a bit of time to do a pencil sketch of the painting and it helped me really *look* at the painting properly. Had I not been trying to copy the painting so precisely, I would never have noticed the skeleton was missing its left thumb. How strange! Did the artist *mean* to do that? I bet Jake would have a theory about the missing thumb.

And another strange thing is that I could swear those two new dinner men from school, Barry and Larry, were at the gallery too. They weren't wearing their white hats and beard nets, but from the great, hulking size of them, I'm sure it was them! I tried to get a decent look at them, but Mum and Dad _suddenly_ decided they were in a rush to get to the Falkirk Fish Festival in time for the Star Starfish Award, so I wasn't able to say hello. I do feel sorry for Mum and Dad. I wonder if they ever will accept that SEABERT is gone and that we no longer have to attend those ridiculous competitions any more – but you said this will help with their healing, so maybe it's worth continuing to go to those things, just for a little while.

In fact, we rushed out of the gallery so quickly, we forgot to pick up my backpack, which Mum had INSISTED I put in the cloakroom. I didn't even want to take it in the first place. So now we have to go back tomorrow. Don't tell Dad, but I'm secretly glad because it gets me more time in the gallery!

Love, *Mia*

Dear Granny,

You'll never guess what happened today! Not only did I get to visit a gallery for the SECOND TIME EVER (the fact that it was the same gallery I visited for the first time only yesterday is neither here nor there), I think I also FOILED a THEFT!

SO, we went back to the gallery to get my backpack and Mum and Dad seemed to be in a strange mood because they suggested I spend some time in the ...

DA DA DAHHHHHH!

GIFT SHOP!!

Dad looked to be coming down with something because

he was dead jumpy and his face was all sweaty, so they left me in the shop while they went to find the toilets. BUT, while I was on my own, I noticed Barry and Larry in the gallery AGAIN. Well, they might not have been Barry and Larry, but they were definitely the same men as I saw yesterday. THAT'S DEAD

116

BARRY?

SUSPICIOUS, I thought – I mean, why would you visit the same gallery for two days in a row (except if, like me, you'd left something in the cloakroom, which is the only plausible explanation for anyone being there two days in a row and, for me, was a TOTAL accident)? I remembered

LARRY?

what you'd said about keeping my eyes open, Granny, so I told a guard about the dodgy men. Next thing I knew, security guards appeared from who-knows-where, and the two massive man-mountains were getting wrestled to the floor! It was very exciting! Such a shame Mum and Dad missed it.

We all got ushered out of the building and finally Mum and Dad found me there. Dad was looking relieved (I don't even want to KNOW what he did in the toilet) and I think they must have looked for me in the shop because they'd got a package with them – I hope they've bought me some art! Wouldn't it be wonderful if this trip had stopped my parents seeing arty pictures as "frivolous clutter"?

I can't wait to get back to school tomorrow and tell Mr Carpsucker about our trip to see *Time Bowing to Death*. And, if I can get up the nerve to speak to them, I'll have to tell Barry and Larry about their DOPPELGANGERS at the gallery – I bet they'll find that super funny! They might even stop GLARING at everyone, just for a moment.

Love, Mia

It's a Mystery!

By Gerta Lowdaviss
The Daily News

Notorious Thieves Caught at Scottish Gallery. Painting Missing

On Sunday 13 November, following a tip-off from a concerned member of the public (an observant child wearing highly distinctive glasses), security guards at the National Galleries, Scotland apprehended two men. These men turned out to be Jonnie and Ronnie Abrahams, two of the notoriously nasty Abrahams gang, wanted for multiple thefts and misdemeanours.

The men were stopped and arrested, but no stolen goods were found on them. However, a painting from the collection *has* gone missing. Cranach the Elder's *Time Bowing to Death* is no longer in its position on the wall of the gallery. While the painting is no **Mona Lisa**, of course, this episode is especially embarrassing for the gallery because its newly installed, state-of-the-art alarm system was never triggered. Police are soliciting any information that could help recover this painting.

View comments

Related Topics

Art	Royal Family	Mona Lisa	Culture

Doctors Report Rise in Headache Sufferers

Local Colpepper GPs, worried about a sudden rise in the number of people suffering from headaches, have called in environmental health experts to check the local water supply and air quality... READ MORE

EYE FOR TRUTH

by Jake Janowski

Loyal readers,

How's this for an interesting bit of news? A painting in a gallery has gone missing! And not just ANY painting, but one *that was once in Lord Colpepper's collection*. Is that not odd? Clearly, as this has been reported in newspapers, the authorities don't believe there to be a link between this stolen painting and The Fish, but I'm not so sure. And the newspaper reported a child with "highly distinctive glasses"? I do hope my friend isn't becoming involved in anything dangerous. If only I could have got further with gathering my dossier of evidence – but I couldn't turn up anything. The authorities really have done a great job of quashing any news stories – until now, at least.

Whatever is going on, I don't think it has anything to do with the strange activities of a certain lizard headmaster. You'll be pleased to hear I have also solved the question of what the strange noise around the school is. That weird, chirruping noise must be...

CRICKETS!

Of course! The lizard-man needs a food source. Thankfully he has not yet developed a taste for human flesh (surely it can't be long) so we should be happy about the crickets. But what will happen when the crickets run out? I need to get the keys and gain access to the east wing, ASAP! Thanks to my stint as the Artful Dodger in last year's production of *Oliver!*, I possess some skills which will come in handy ... but are a bit rusty. Looks like it's time to start picking a pocket or two...

And if you worry that I only write about doom and gloom on this blog, here is a good piece of news: I have a fan! My first real fan! Not just a fan, but a new year eleven pupil who looks like an angel, with eyes of the warmest brown, on a quest for the cold, hard truth.

Hello, Belle Pepper, if you're reading this.

Number of views: 18,462   **Likes:** 6,677

SURVEILLANCE REPORT
by Trainee Agent
Belle Pepper

Initial contact has been made with the target.

Will send progress report shortly.

From: MiaB@StarfishInstructions.net ≡ ✕
To: KBerg55@fjsn.net
Date: 16 November
Subject: I love it when a plan comes together!

Dear Granny,

Mum and Dad seem slightly more relaxed this week. I'd like to think that's the POWER of ART. And, most amazingly of all, they've said they're actually LOOKING FORWARD to our next gallery visit this weekend! I can't wait to get to Tate Liverpool to see the next of Lord Colpepper's pictures!

I thought Mum and Dad would still want to visit an aquarium while we're there - there's a great aquarium at the World Museum in Liverpool - but they haven't even mentioned it. It's probably just as well because Mum made such a scene at the Falkirk Fish Festival, where she sobbed over a tank of starfish and stamped on the floor, wailing, "Seabert, oh Seabert, where are you now, Seabert?" Looks like Mum may have moved on to the anger stage of grief!

Without SEABERT around, I am at least getting more attention, and Mum's even booked me on to a drawing workshop that the gallery is holding for local schoolchildren (even though I'm not local - but who's going to check?). I really hope I get a chance to look at Turner's *Sketch of a Broken Skeleton (Left Hand)* close up and maybe even sketch it. Even if school didn't appreciate my talent for art, I shouldn't let that stop me!

I nearly went to tell Jake about our gallery trip as he's always been so supportive of my interest in art, but he was too busy with his *new friend* to notice. Just who is Belle Pepper anyway? And why is her uniform so crisp and perfect?

Love, *Mia*

From: KBerg55@fjsn.net

To: MiaB@StarfishInstructions.net

Date: 17 November

Subject: G'day from Australia

___

Dearest Mia,

You've got the gallery bug! I'm so pleased you enjoyed your first visits, and how exciting that you stopped a theft! Well done for being so observant! And what super news about your upcoming visit. You'll love the workshop, I'm sure. Drawing the works in front of you will help you see the art in a totally new light. And you won't believe how hungry concentrating will make you – I hope they're ordering food in for the workshop. I must have food on the brain. Here in Melbourne, my latest article has been about children and healthy eating: ***Kids Make Healthy Snacks***.

Am I sensing a little jealousy that Jake has found a new friend?

Just heading to the salon. Am thinking short and blonde this time. Or pink plaits? XXX

Kat B. | Freelance journalist for science and nature | fjsn.net
Sent from my phone

Dear Granny,

I've just had THE MOST AMAZING DAY! The drawing workshop was super mega awesome! I got to spend the ENTIRE morning sitting with the drawing by JMW Turner in front of me, copying its every detail. No wonder Turner is considered one of England's greatest artists – even in a simple pencil sketch, you can tell he's *really* good! Gail, the Gallery Educator, was super impressed with my drawing – she joked she could barely tell the difference between mine and the real thing. As if my work could be mistaken for a Turner! It was lovely to hear, but, actually, I think you might be right about copying paintings – I'm not sure I learned anything more about myself as an artist. Perhaps real artists *are* those people who express something of themselves through art? Is that why Shanice won the competition instead of me?

You're also right about how concentrating for a long time makes you extra hungry! I felt like I could eat my left arm – which was funny, because

the skeleton in the painting was missing its index finger, exactly as if a very hungry JW Turner had bitten it off after a particularly focused painting session! Thankfully, it must have been lunchtime as all these pizza delivery people appeared. Not just one or two but LOADS of them! Gail was in some kind of panic, wildly clearing up the drawings that had been done in the morning so they didn't get pizza grease on them. Before my drawing could get piled up, a particularly big, hulking delivery person plonked a stack of pizza boxes smack down on it. I shouted at her, and she picked up the boxes and ran out, taking my picture with her!

Well! I wasn't having that, so I chased after her, shouting **"Stop! Thief! Stop that pizza delivery person!"**

Well, next thing I knew, security guards were piling on ALL the poor pizza delivery people from every direction. Turns out, if you shout "Stop! Thief!" in a gallery, people think that **actual real art** is being stolen, so the police were a bit grumpy (to say the least) when they found out it was

an eleven-year-old's drawing that had been snatched. At least I got my drawing back (although it is a bit greasy).

I don't really know where Mum and Dad disappeared off to at this point (my money is on the toilet, as Dad had been complaining about his nervy tummy again), but Dad was clutching a pizza box when we met back up and STILL has it with him now. YUCK - toilet pizza! I hope he doesn't try to eat it. Or maybe Dad thinks it's a piece of modern art? Well, it worked for Andy Warhol, I guess.

Love, *Mia*

PS I'm ignoring your Jake comment. I'm not jealous of anything. I'm happy Jake has found a friend who shares his interests. Good luck to them, I say. And don't be thinking that me commenting here is a sign that I feel otherwise because I don't. And that's my final word on the matter.

Pizza Pandemonium at Tate Liverpool

By Gerta Lowdaviss
The Daily News

Police were called to Tate Liverpool today following strange goings-on with an art workshop for local schoolchildren and the surprising simultaneous delivery of two hundred pizzas by twenty delivery riders.

"I must have mistakenly added an extra zero to my order," sobbed Gail, the Gallery Educator responsible for the event. "I don't even like pizza – I'm lactose intolerant," she wailed.

To make matters worse, one of the delivery riders was accused of stealing a work of art, which led to the lockdown of the gallery and a person-by-person search of each delivery rider. Unfortunately, this turned out to be a complete waste of police time as the "work of art" stolen was an eleven-year-old's drawing (although the officer who found it had to admit it was very good).

The strangeness of this case does not end there: of the twenty delivery riders held and searched, the one found to have taken the child's drawing has been identified as Bonnie Abrahams, a well-known art thief and one of the unbelievably unpleasant Abrahams gang. After stealing a *child's* drawing, we are fairly confident this Abrahams's notoriety as an art thief is at an end.

And, strangest of all, in the confusion, it appears that the work of art being used during Gail's drawing workshop – a sketch by JMW Turner – has *actually* gone missing. "If anyone accidentally picked up this priceless drawing instead of their own work, please contact the gallery as soon as possible. My successor will be waiting to hear from you," howled the unfortunate Gail.

View comments

Related Topics

| Art | Royal Family | Mona Lisa | Culture |

One Month Remaining to Find *The Lost Mona Lisa*

It's becoming increasingly unlikely that anyone will be able to claim the £25 million reward for finding *The Lost Mona Lisa* as time is ticking away and only a month remains… READ MORE

Mr and Mrs Berghler,

Well done so far. Two jobs down, three to go.
   Starfish is safe for now, but remember: if you
fail, it won't only be me you're letting down.

Dear Granny,

There's so much going on at the moment, I don't know where to start.

The BIG NEWS is that Mum and Dad ALLOWED me to stick ON THE WALL OF OUR LIVING ROOM my sketch of Turner's *Broken Skeleton!* (Well, I don't mean that it's a sketch of JMW Turner's actual bones, but my drawing inspired by his sketch – you know what I mean!) It actually looks rather nice alongside all the diagrams of aquatic creatures, like a reminder that we are all animals, basically made of the same stuff.

I think they're starting to cope much better with SEABERT being gone; they've even started new hobbies! They attended a trial limbo-dancing session at the local community centre, although I think maybe they've realized they're a bit old and unbendy for that. And they're now doing loads of yoga every evening before tea. The good thing is that they're doing these things **together** and, even though I know they're still sad about SEABERT, they just seem to be being nicer to each other, which seems to be making them happier than they've been for a long time.

AND, very excitingly, we've just announced the trip to take my

PETITION to London – TOOT! TOOT! Come on, December 19! I can't wait. Mr Rothering's been super helpful and Shanice has also been great. We're going to take her petition against the name Colpepper along too. My **PETITION** has reached a grand total of *85,766*, so I'm feeling confident that we'll make the 100,000 mark in time to hand it in to Parliament, and then the Members of Parliament will surely HAVE to debate it. Ha! Who needs Mr Chimaera MP? Mum and Dad have even jumped

at the chance of helping with the trip. They said they *really* wanted to go. Actually, no, they said they really NEEDED to go. They're really keen to support me, which is so great. Mum even suggested this would be an opportunity to go to the National Gallery and see the Rubens picture from the Colpepper Hall collection. She remembered! Mum remembered something I am interested in, something entirely unrelated to starfish!

Miss Tench has somehow managed to work out her budget so we can head to London with all our instruments on a coach – although Shanice did point out that using trains would be far more eco-friendly! We'll sound really good when we're doing our busking. We just need to pick a spot that's nice and central and that attracts lots of crowds. I was wondering about outside the Houses of Parliament, but Miss Tench worried we might be seen as a **security threat**. Any ideas? I haven't really had time to do much practising myself at home, but thankfully my part tends to go *Bom Bom Bom Bom* so hopefully I can manage that.

Jake hasn't been turning up to orchestra practice lately. I guess the kazoo is pretty easy but, still, for the sake of the orchestra, he should show more commitment. Whenever I do see him now, he always seems to be with perfect Belle Pepper, staring up at her with soppy, puppy-dog eyes. Bleurgh!

Love, *Mia*

PS Mum and Dad have also told me they've planned a SURPRISE for this weekend. Oh, please don't let it be a new starfish...!

EYE FOR TRUTH

by Jake Janowski

Have you ever noticed how beautiful the sunrise is? Birds are tweeting, and the air feels fresh.

Even Mr Scales is looking less scaly at the moment.

And so what if paintings by artists long-dead are being stolen?

It's a good time to be alive!

Number of views: 31,822   **Likes:** 423

SURVEILLANCE REPORT

by Trainee Agent

Belle Pepper

Progress limited by target apparently developing feelings for me. Have been unable to get any sense out of him at all. Or, for several days now, even words. My presence appears to be a distraction from his conspiracy theories. If only I could offer him something to get him back on track. Looking back through his old blogs, the target wants evidence regarding The Fish's unreported activities. Could this be provided to him? Perhaps, in return for gaining his trust with evidence, he'll share the name of The Fish with me?

Comms from

Agent Carrot

Trainee Agent Belle Pepper,
Agreed. Am putting together a file that you can share with the target when the time is right. For now, hang back and avoid further contact.

Louvre Offers Loan of "Real" *Mona Lisa* to Royal Family

By Gerta Lowdaviss
The Daily News

While the search for *The Lost Mona Lisa* continues and enters the final couple of weeks for the £25 million reward to be claimed, the Director of the Louvre has jokingly offered to lend *The Mona Lisa* to the British royal family – for the bargain price of £24 million! The Louvre in Paris is the biggest museum in the world and houses many thousands of priceless works of art along its miles of corridors. Its star exhibit is their version of *The Mona Lisa*, for which crowds gather every day.

In a move likely to sour relations between France and England, the Louvre's Director is reported to have said, "If the British royal family, so foolish to misplace their treasured version of *The Mona Lisa* long ago, is so desperate for a copy of Leonardo da Vinci's masterpiece, they are welcome to borrow our version for a few months."

A spokesperson for the palace responded by saying that the royal family understood the offer to be a joke and that the Louvre can shove... READ MORE

View comments

Related Topics

| Art | Royal Family | Mona Lisa | Culture |

From: MiaB@StarfishInstructions.net ≡ ×

To: KBerg55@fjsn.net

Date: 2 December

Subject: It was NOT a starfish! WOOT WOOT

Dear Granny,

Mum and Dad are taking me to the National Museum Wales in Cardiff for a SLEEPOVER!

WOW! Only three weeks ago, I had my first visit EVER to a gallery – and now I'm going to SPEND THE NIGHT in one!

It's so kind of Mum and Dad to do this for me when they're still grieving over their *STARFISH*. I overheard them talking, and Mum said, "If we go along to this gallery, we'll be one step closer to being back with *SEABERT*."

I guess Mum must be on to the bargaining stage of grief?

Anyway, we're heading to Wales tomorrow, so I should pack now and get some sleep – hopefully I won't be getting much tomorrow night. I'M SO EXCITED!!

Love, *Mia*

PS My *PETITION* now has OVER 90,000 signatures. This has been a great week!

PPS I do feel a bit sorry for Shanice, whose petition only has 3,566. I believe her petition is **really important,** but maybe, for most people, they don't really think about *who* a statue is of, or *why* something is named after someone – but they *should,* because otherwise what kind of messages do these tributes give out for future generations?

EYE FOR TRUTH

by Jake Janowski

Oh, loyal readers.

Thank you for sticking by me.

Thank you for not deserting me.

Why are humans designed with such tender hearts? How do we cope with the rush and excitement of love one day and then the abject horror of rejection the next? I am telling myself that it is just a chemical imbalance in the brain, but, in truth, my heart is broken.

There is nothing for it. To mend this broken heart I must throw myself back into my missions – luckily for you, my faithful seekers of the truth.

Forget what I wrote before, "Scaly" Scales is now looking more and more lizard-like by the day. His skin is so dry it makes me want to coat him in cream. If he is transforming from man to lizard, surely this transformation will be complete soon? *Then* what will happen?

Nothing good, you can be certain of that.

If I'm the only one seeing this change, I'm the only one who can DO SOMETHING ABOUT IT. I have started Operation Pick a Pocket or Two in and around school, and the old skills are returning. I have managed to snaffle several sweets, Mr Carpsucker's comb, and a pair of glasses. The glasses gave me a headache as soon as I put them on – *of course*. Unfortunately, I didn't keep them long enough to work out the mind-control technology certainly embedded within; I felt too guilty, so I returned everything, completely unnoticed.

But I think I'm ready for the *big one,* the one I won't feel guilty about: Mr Scales's bunch of keys. Whatever he's *really* doing in the art department, I *will* find out.

And is it just me, or are there fewer hulking clones around the school now? What's been happening to them? Maybe, like all clones, they're defective and only have a short lifespan.

Or *maybe* they're becoming the first victims of Mr Scales?

OR, and you may think this is far-fetched even for me, *maybe* they're something to do with the recently reported art heists! Clones appearing at Colpepper Hall School just as pieces of art from Lord Colpepper's collection start to go missing from galleries? Those members of the notoriously nasty Abrahams gang who are getting arrested do look remarkably like our new school staff.

Could they be in cahoots with The Fish?

I do worry about my friend – she's too close to all this for my liking and my already damaged heart would shatter completely if she was in trouble.

SURVEILLANCE REPORT

by Trainee Agent

Belle Pepper

New appraoch seems to be working. I have started
to ignore our target, and he now seems to be back
on track with his blog and theories. He keeps
mentioning a friend, but I have never seen him with
anyone at school.

Could there be some truth in the target's theory
about a link between the Abrahams gang and The Fish?
Perhaps this is a lead we can follow?

Any progress on the dossier of evidence? If I can
present him with something to back up his theories,
he may still open up to me.

From: MiaB@StarfishInstructions.net ☰ ✕
To: KBerg55@fjsn.net
Date: 3 December
Subject: Tappety tap tap

Dear Granny,

I am EXHAUSTED, but we've had SO MUCH FUN tonight that I wanted to write to you while I remember it all.

There were **loads** of families who'd signed up for the gallery sleepover, and it was BRILLIANT to be surrounded by people who love art. Me and Mum and Dad turned up already in our pyjamas, which was dead embarrassing as apparently you were not expected to do that; changing rooms had been provided. It meant I had to spend all evening in my *STARFISH* onesie - but that, combined with my "striking" glasses, at least got people noticing me, and I was then able to ask them to sign my petition - YAY! I don't know where Mum and Dad got their new pyjamas from - they were very skin-tight and black and really did not leave much to the imagination, if you get what I mean!

The visit started out with us getting a tour of the museum using torches, which was AMAZING because it created a whole different atmosphere and everything suddenly looked far more dramatic. The

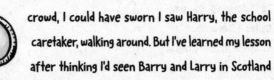

flickering light really does play tricks on your mind: in the crowd, I could have sworn I saw Harry, the school caretaker, walking around. But I've learned my lesson after thinking I'd seen Barry and Larry in Scotland – just my overactive imagination firing on all cylinders!

Tahir, our guide, toured our group through the back staff offices, which was SO COOL, as I bet hardly anyone ever gets to see behind the scenes. We even got taken into the security office, so we could see all the screens playing the views from all the cameras. Mum said something about recognizing the "Verisafe Alarm 3000" alarm system, which made her sound really nerdy and embarrassing, but the security guard was clearly impressed. He even started talking about security details that I'm not sure he should have shared with us. Like, do you know that galleries perform a secret monthly audit to check that their paintings haven't been swapped for fakes by some thief called The Fish? That's the kind of fact that Jake would love. Maybe I will tell him when I next see him. But he's always just obsessing over that year eleven nowadays, so maybe I won't. Argh! Why have you made me feel like even mentioning Jake's name is a great big sign that I miss him? It's not, you know. It's just – erm – habit?

Anyway, back in the galleries, Tahir shone an infrared light around and you could see all the laser security beams zig-zagging across the room, like a twinkly light show for fairies. It was so mesmerizing that I almost missed Poussin's *Landscape with Death* painting, tucked behind a big column actually IN the gallery with all the lasers. I told Tahir all about my

project on the Colpepper Hall collection and he winked, got out his walkie-talkie, messaged the security guard and - CLICK - like magic, the laser beams disappeared and the proper lights came up ... and I was allowed to look at the painting!

It is a good painting, but I'm starting to think that all this OLD art isn't really for me. It doesn't feel particularly relevant. Who would want a painting of a landscape with a skeleton in it? I guess Lord Colpepper did. That's the good thing about galleries - I can learn about what I like and what I don't like, and my taste seems different from Lord Colpepper's!

Back at the education centre of the museum, we got to create our own art. Even Mum and Dad threw themselves into it. Turns out Dad is quite a good artist when he tries. Maybe you do have things in common after all! He cracked open some paints and tried to recreate the Poussin painting we'd been looking at - and, I have to say, he didn't do a bad job. Mum had a much more "creative" approach and glued red sparkly strings across black card. She was SO focused on her artwork, she was in her own little world. I knew what she was doing - creating a picture of the twinkly laser beams. She was concentrating so hard, it was like she was trying to place each strand in EXACTLY the right place. Who knew my parents were so artistic!

Everyone's buzzing with excitement, so it is taking ages to get to sleep, which is why I'm emailing you - good job Mum packed my DoodlepadX500, or I would

be mega bored now. Dad has got that jittery, sweaty look
again, so I hope he doesn't have tummy trouble during
the night.

I should go now, people are starting to tut when I tap
with the stylus.

Like now.

And now.

And.

And.

Ha – I'm just doing this to annoy them now!

OK.

Better go.

Love, *Mia*

National Museum of Wales Sleepover Hit By Theft

By Gerta Lowdaviss
The Daily News

The National Museum of Wales, Cardiff, has had one of the jewels of its collection, *Landscape with Death* by Nicholas Poussin, stolen during a sleepover event. The thief replaced the painting with a forgery so poor it looks like a child has done it. Once the theft was noticed, security tapes of the sleepover event were searched and the familiar figure of Connie Abrahams was identified and arrested. As yet, she is keeping silent about the whereabouts of the stolen painting. The criminally crooked Abrahams gang certainly has been busy these last few weeks. Where might they strike next?

Additionally, this theft is the third such where the state-of-the-art Verisafe Alarm 3000 gallery alarm system failed to activate, leading galleries up and down the country to reassess their security services. The security manager of the National Museum of Wales told us, "Intuitive, plug-in, ready-to-go systems such as the Verisafe Alarm 3000 are all well and good, but this theft has highlighted that the gallery has been left vulnerable. What we really need is an alarm system with professionally written instructions that we can properly understand."

The Verisafe Alarm company was contacted for comment, but we only got through to an answerphone message.

"These days, maybe *The Lost Mona Lisa* is safer being just that: lost," mused the security manager.

View comments

Related Topics

| Art | Royal Family | Mona Lisa | Culture |

EYE FOR TRUTH

by Jake Janowski

Hello again, faithful followers.

Yet again, EYE FOR TRUTH is able to reveal a discovery that others have been too blind to notice...

Another Colpepper painting gone missing, with another member of the Abrahams gang arrested? Clearly, the Abrahams are being used as stooges while *someone else* gets away with stealing picture after picture after picture! And, even if the authorities haven't worked this out, you all KNOW who I think is behind this.

Perhaps the authorities are missing this **OBVIOUS** link because The Fish normally targets mega-star, show-stopping paintings and Lord Colpepper's pictures are not quite in that league, even if the works are by important artists. So what is the reason for The Fish to go after these? I believe, dear readers, that there is sentimental value attached to the Lord Colpepper paintings for The Fish because – and how's this for an EYE FOR TRUTH exclusive – The Fish attended Colpepper Hall School! There is a direct link between the paintings that are going missing and The Fish! But even for the most ardent fan or alumnus of Colpepper Hall School, stealing Lord Colpepper's paintings seems like an odd move. Something isn't adding up, but my ability to spot a conspiracy tells me I'm completely right about the identity of The Fish, which makes me worry all the more about my friend.

I see from the comments that some of you out there think I should tell my suspicions to the police. But what will they say?

"Oh, it's that boy with his RIDICULOUS ideas – what is it this time? More mind-control nonsense?"

They're not going to believe me, are they? And even if they did, why would I want to get The Fish arrested, **ESPECIALLY** when my best friend could be involved? So, for now, I'll have to wait and watch. But don't worry, I have other FISH to fry (excuse the pun)...

How's this as a teaser for my next blog: I managed to pick Mr Scales's pocket and I have the key!!!! (As well as some dried crickets – yuck.)

In the next exciting instalment of EYE FOR TRUTH, I should be able to reveal ALL.

Number of views: 42,776   **Likes:** 18,362

Comms from

Agent Carrot

Trainee Agent Belle Pepper,

No credible link found between The Fish and the Abrahams gang. Even though they're in custody, these hardened criminals are not likely to crack under interrogation.

And the evidence for the dossier is proving difficult to gather, as we suppressed the information so successfully. Sifting through redacted reports now. Dossier should be with you in the next few days.

Dearest Mia,

I'm so sorry it's been a while since I messaged. I've been very busy writing up an article on over-population *(Babies To Blame for Population Growth)*, not to mention my water-divining course here in Prague. But it sounds like there's lots going on for you, too. My goodness, how exciting! All of these gallery visits with your parents AND your trip to London coming up. Wasn't it super of your mum to suggest going to the National Gallery? Do you know, that's my favourite gallery in London? They used to run a project where they would lend paintings to schools – I wonder what happened to that. If you do manage to visit the gallery, Trafalgar Square, just outside it, would be the perfect place for busking.

With your plans really coming on for taking your petition to London, wouldn't it be great to get it covered by a newspaper? I would do it myself, but your wonderful petition doesn't exactly fall under the category of science or nature! For all its faults, the *Colpepper Online Gazette* would probably be the best publication for the story.

What a shame you've fallen out with Jake. Although, it's never too late to reconnect with a good friend, even if you feel they've now moved on.

I'm so pleased your parents are doing better. Losing Seabert was always going to be hard, but it all seems to be turning out for the best. I'm glad they're now focusing more on your interests – as they should! And I'm so delighted to hear that your trips to galleries are making you start to think about your tastes and all the different painting styles out there.

About to nip to the shops – I'm suddenly out of shaving foam. XXX

Kat B. | Freelance journalist for science and nature | fjsn.net
Sent from my phone

Dear Granny,

Guess what? Mum and Dad have WON A COMPETITION to visit the National Gallery of Ireland! Isn't that incredible? AMAZINGLY, that's where the other picture is from Lord Colpepper's collection - *Winter Scene* by Brueghel the Younger. I didn't even realize they entered competitions that weren't starfish-related! It's for four people, so I've invited Shanice along too.

The strange thing is, I'd said to Mum and Dad that maybe we didn't need to see the Lord Colpepper picture that is in Ireland. They've been so great over the last few weeks and I've loved visiting galleries with them, but I know their business isn't doing well so I was starting to worry about the expense of travelling over to Dublin. They looked even more disappointed than me at the idea of not going, so this out-of-the-blue competition win is good news all round!

Shanice and I are going to plan our gallery visit to see how many works of art we can spot that *aren't* by old white men! It's sad that most of the very famous artists from the past are just that - white and male. All of the artists who created Lord Colpepper's five paintings were white and male. I know it was a very different time when Lord Colpepper was alive – but where were the women artists then? Where were the different cultures? Surely they existed back then? At least other people have more of a chance these days, I hope! It's amazing how my visits to galleries have got me thinking not just about my taste in art, but also about which artists are represented on the walls.

It's less than TWO WEEKS to go until the London trip. And my **PETITION** is *nearly at* 100,000 *signatures* – PHEW! BUT I tried to get Mr and Mrs Janowski interested in covering the **PETITION** and the trip for the *Colpepper Online Gazette*, and they said I wasn't thinking BIG ENOUGH and that if they were going to cover it in the newspaper it would need to have a fun twist. I don't know whether they were just giving excuses because they know I've fallen out with Jake, or if they really meant it – but they seemed to think the story would be better if I was THINKING BIGGER. What does that even mean?

It's starting to feel a bit overwhelming, to be honest, like the responsibility of all future arts education rests with my **PETITION**. You're right that all I can do is raise awareness and get as many signatures as possible – but what if it fails? What if I can't persuade the government to fund arts education properly? What if parliament refuses to debate it? What hope would there be for me and others like me if it doesn't work? I don't really see our headteacher doing much to help either. No one sees him any more, even though a demolition crew has started to set up outside the east wing! Whatever plans Mr Scales

HAVE YOU

SEEN HIM?

had to stop the school governors bulldozing the east wing into a car park don't seem to have come to anything. I wish I could talk to Jake about this – even if he had a ridiculous theory about what was going on, it would at least be fun to hear.

Have I told you that we're now studying the Ancient Greeks in history? For history that long ago, it's difficult to tell what is real and what is made up. I mean, this story all about the Trojan horse – can that really have happened? People hiding in a statue of a horse? Very far-fetched if you ask me.

Love, Mia

Dearest Mia,

I LOVED learning about the Ancient Greeks when I was younger, and I'm so pleased you now know how bonkers the story of the Trojan Horse is. Such an ingenious way to get into a tricky place! My goodness, you are learning so much. And it sounds like these gallery visits are really helping shape your taste in art – it's good to know what you don't like, as well as what you do! How marvellous. You should definitely look into new work that is being created at the moment. There are loads of interesting contemporary works, projects, awards, events – surely you're seeing this just from visiting the museums and seeing how they're encouraging children and audiences to engage with art?

My personal favourite is the *Fourth Plinth* project which, funnily enough, is in Trafalgar Square in London. When the square was originally designed, the four plinths in its four corners were supposed to carry statues. Three of them were completed, but the fourth one remained empty. Everyone believes that this was due to a lack of money to complete the statue, but I've heard a rumour that the *Fourth Plinth*, which just *happens* to be at the corner nearest to the National Gallery, remained empty because it contains a secret underground entrance to the National Gallery! There! That's a theory even your Jake would be proud of!

Must sign off as I'm in Bengaluru and due at Barbara Burramundi's for my latest astrological chart reading. As a fellow Pisces, I'm sure you understand that the world contains a mysticism that science alone cannot explain. And, after that, I must put the finishing touches to my latest article: ***Scientists Discover Reason for Tigers' Stripes: To Avoid Being Spotted****. XXX

Kat B. | Freelance journalist for science and nature | fjsn.net
Sent from my phone

GENIUS GRANNY!

I'd never HEARD of the *Fourth Plinth* project, but you're right – it's BRILLIANT.
What an excellent way to use that empty space in Trafalgar Square. I've
looked at the sculptures they've chosen to display there and they're so
awesome, inspiring – and fun! I contacted the organizers to get more
information and told them all about my petition. We're going to London on
December 19th to give the PETITION to Parliament, visit the National
Gallery *and* busk in Trafalgar Square. And it turns out that December 19th
will be the ONE DAY over the next EIGHT YEARS when the plinth will be empty!

That might sound like really bad luck, BUT Laurence, the guy I spoke to,
was so interested in my PETITION and so worried about funding for
the arts that he said he could maybe get me up on the plinth for a photo
shoot about the PETITION !

HOW'S THAT FOR THINKING BIGGER?

I'm going to be taken up there on a cherry picker! If I'm lucky, I might
even get to check out whether there really IS a secret passage from there
to the National Gallery. Ha ha! Watch this space!

And this means that even the *Colpepper Online Gazette* is on board now. Mum is really excited for me and has suggested that we create some kind of sculpture to be up there with me, otherwise I could look really teeny-tiny up there by myself. I'm amazed she's got the time to offer to do this, since she and Dad have now taken up aerial acrobatics. They've really taken to it and have even set up ropes and hoops hanging in the backyard. It makes me too nervous to watch them, but I have to admit they're pretty graceful.

Teeny

Anyway, Mum is determined to help, so she's papier-mâchéing away in the garage. I *really* want to know what she's making, but she just keeps telling me that what she's doing is a surprise for London.

Tomorrow morning we're heading over to Ireland, ready to visit the National Gallery of Ireland on Saturday. Shanice is really looking forward to it and has planned our gallery route, which is really helping me out because I'm just focused on London and my brain can't really compute anything more at the moment.

Love, *Mia*

PS My **PETITION** has now OFFICIALLY clicked over to MORE THAN **100,000** signatures!

WOOT WOOT!

EYE FOR TRUTH

by Jake Janowski

Are you ready for this, people?

I have seen the truth WITH MY OWN EYES.

And I was RIGHT.

I was right about everything.

There IS a lizard man living amongst us, and his name is MR SCALES.

The east wing of Colpepper Hall School is FULL of tanks: some full of insects and others empty, so probably waiting for – *goodness knows what!*

Row upon row of tanks, lit by the soft glow of heat lamps. And in the centre of the room, what looks like a sunbed – *or is it some kind of transformation chamber?*

I did not have time to investigate further as I heard someone coming – so I need to return and gather evidence in order to inform the authorities. Uncovering the truth is a dangerous business. And if this is the last you hear from me, look for me in the art department of Colpepper Hall School. I may have become lizard food – or, worse, lizard boy – by the time I'm found.

Number of views: 45,833   **Likes:** 25,373

Dear Granny,

Finally, I'M able to email YOU from a different country! Now you're not the only jet-setter in the family.

It turned out that the day of our trip to the National Gallery of Ireland was not just any normal day, it was a big event to celebrate the opening of their latest exhibition called *FUN! Entertainments, Celebrations and Gatherings*, so there were special activities going on all over the place. Shanice knew about this from her online research but had kept it as a surprise for me. It REALLY brought the whole museum to life! Actors were wandering around in fancy costumes, musicians were performing in all corners of the galleries, and there were even circus performers, some of whom were doing high-wire tricks in the large entrance hall. Shanice and I giggled when we spotted someone who looked exactly like Garry from our year dressed as a circus strongman, complete with slicked-down hair and painted-on moustache. With his great, hulking size, the real Garry would *definitely* make a great strongman!

Not Garry

Garry

Mum and Dad seem exhausted, which is understandable, as work seems to be picking up; they keep getting contacted by art galleries wanting to change from their Verisafe Alarm systems! All my parents wanted to do, therefore, was sit in the café (although Dad was AGAIN looking jittery and nervous, so I'm not sure how wise hanging out by food really was) - but they were happy for me and Shanice to head off by ourselves into the exhibition, which was the first thing Shanice had planned for us to visit.

Brueghel the Younger's *Winter Scene* from Colpepper Hall was there. It's such a strange painting - it looks like a celebration, with people in an oldy-worldy village all enjoying skating on a frozen lake, but then you realize that the villagers are being led by a skeleton, who is freezing over the land, which would probably be very scary for the villagers, except he has four fingers - AGAIN! The detail in it is minute but, because of the amount of people in the gallery, it was difficult to get up much closer. The painting had been hung next to *The Peasant's Wedding* by the same artist, which was definitely a much happier scene. We went back to the café to tell Mum and Dad about having seen the painting, but there was no sign of them. You know *exactly* where I think they'd got to (poor Dad and his dodgy tummy)...

Just as we left the exhibition space, the power WENT OUT around the whole gallery and everything was plunged into darkness! Everyone started screaming and rushing for the exits. In the mayhem, I lost my glasses (NOT MY FAULT!), so Shanice had to guide me around. When Mum and Dad appeared out of the gallery, I almost didn't recognize them (not helped, of course, by the whole no-glasses thing) because they were wearing gallery security staff uniforms! Apparently they'd spilled drink on themselves and gallery staff had kindly offered to loan them some clothes.

I never did find my glasses, so not only am I really struggling to see anything, I'm also sad that my unique glasses are no more. Shanice was brilliant at helping me, but I'm sorry we didn't get to see more of the gallery, although maybe it's just as well because Shanice was starting to get one of her headaches.

Love, *Mia*

Donnie Abrahams, Leader of the Flagrantly Foul Abrahams Gang, Arrested in Ireland

By Gerta Lowdaviss
The Daily News

The fifth and final member of the truly terrible Abrahams gang is behind bars today, following yet another art heist, this time at the National Gallery of Ireland.

In a bustling, brilliant day of celebrations at the gallery, Donnie Abrahams took the opportunity to steal *two* paintings by Pieter Brueghel the Younger. One painting, *The Peasant's Wedding,* was found strapped to Donnie's considerable middle – but its sister painting, *Winter Scene,* is nowhere to be found. If Donnie Abrahams had the opportunity to pass the painting on to an accomplice, he's not telling. The only thing Donnie is quoted as saying is, "I did not mean to take THAT ONE."

Many questions surround this incident. Police picked up Donnie after a member of the public reported seeing a "circus performer" acting suspiciously during a high-wire act during a chaotic moment in the gallery when the lighting failed. Police tried to get Donnie to demonstrate how he used the high wire to access the painting, but the wire snapped under Donnie's considerable weight and he plunged several feet to the floor. The police then discovered two gallery guards locked in a cupboard in only their underwear. Donnie Abrahams claims not to have had anything to do with them, but the police are nonetheless certain they've got their man.

So the art world can rest more easily tonight, with the entire Abrahams gang locked up. However, in each case, a picture is still missing. If you have any information about the whereabouts of the stolen pictures, don't protect the horrible Abrahams gang – we'd love to hear from you.

View comments

Related Topics

| Art | Royal Family | Mona Lisa | Culture |

Museums Cash In!

Museums and galleries around the country are making the most of their bumper visitor figures to plan increasingly ambitious public programmes, from sleepover nights to exhibition extravaganzas... READ MORE

To Codename Iris

Well done. Four paintings collected so far, and just the Rubens in the National Gallery to go. I knew I could trust you. Let me know when to expect the fifth, and *The Lost Mona Lisa* will be as good as ~~mine~~ ours. And just in the nick of time!

 Good work.

Codename Boss Eye

To Codename Boss Eye

MC Glasses

22 High Street, Colpepper

I'm sorry, I don't think it is wise for us to be
in contact.
    Isn't that what you said?
    And isn't it odd that at every turn there seems
to have been a completely different team working
on stealing the skeleton keys, even though I was
the only one tasked with retrieving them? Do you
know anything about that?
    I appear to have been doing rather well without
your help or involvement. So well, in fact, that
I may just claim the reward myself.
    I don't know you, and you have nothing to do
with this.

Codename Iris

Dear Granny,

It is officially only SIX DAYS until we head to London. SO EXCITING!!!!

It's really coming together and – can you believe it? – my "actions" over the summer seem now to have been forgiven by Mr Michael Chimaera because...

Drum roll, please...

He rang us yesterday and OFFERED to present MY PETITION to Parliament!!

HOW GREAT IS THAT?

It will REALLY help get more attention for my PETITION to have a Member of Parliament show so much support for it. He's EVEN offered to GIVE me some new replacement glasses! (I wonder how he heard that I lost mine?) That is super helpful of him, as I am currently really struggling to see without my glasses, and it would be such a shame to see London just as a furry blob!

So maybe Michael Chimaera is not so bad after all.

There is ONE teensy, tiny problem though: he's said he doesn't want to present Shanice's petition about changing the name of the school and town from Colpepper. He told me that it would just WEAKEN my own **PETITION** if it was paired up with hers. It seems really mean for Mr Chimaera to talk about his own granddaughter's work like that, but, as a Member of Parliament, he must know what he's talking about and have my best interests at heart, surely. But he wanted ME to tell Shanice. BUM .

So I found Shanice in the music department, although she was playing the violin, not the flute, which I thought was a bit weird. Anyway, I got through my whole explanation about not including her **PETITION** when we go to London and that I'm very sorry and I wish there was something I could do and I hope she wasn't that upset and that she's still my friend and that I wanted to give her a hug.

Turns out I was talking to Brianna, who does **NOT** have a **PETITION** and does **NOT** care about me being sorry and was **NOT** upset and definitely still does **NOT** want a hug from me.

When I did eventually find Shanice, Brianna had already told her (thanks, Brianna) and she was most definitely in a huff. Sometimes you don't need to be able to see properly to see that someone is annoyed with you. The storming off is a pretty big clue.

I was so pleased to get to the end of the day and was really touched to see Mum appear at the school gates to pick me up. So I rushed to give her a hug. Nope. Turns out it was Brianna again.

That girl *really* does not like me.

I'll be so glad when I pick up my new glasses from Mr Chimaera tomorrow.

Love, *Mia*

EYE FOR TRUTH

by Jake Janowski

Faithful followers,

This blog is called ***EYE FOR TRUTH*** because I can see things that other people miss, things that *aren't quite right*. I have the ability to see a problem, a mystery, a **conspiracy**.

I spotted something wasn't *quite right* when I first saw Mr Scales – and how right was I? I haven't had a chance to get back into the art department, but we now all know the truth, don't we? I also saw danger when my friend got glasses from MC Glasses. I KNOW there's something dodgy about MC Glasses and Michael Chimaera. And look who's suddenly got himself on the trip to London? Surely he's only doing it for the good publicity it will bring him. All that hard work by my brilliant, talented friend – and the glory will go to Michael Chimaera. I suspect that he heard about the photo shoot on the Fourth Plinth and realized it would be good publicity for him to be seen to be involved. But what does Michael Chimaera *really* want?

But today, I find myself with a knot in my stomach. I have always trusted my eyes, but what is my stomach trying to tell me?

In my hands, I hold a sealed dossier – delivered to me by an angel. An angel with grey knee-high socks and an unquenchable thirst for the answers!

And what does this dossier contain? I hear you cry.

According to that grey-socked seraphim, it contains evidence about The Fish's unreported activities over the years.

And the price I had to pay for this evidence was to give a name.

Was that a fair swap?

Or have I been tricked into betraying the family of my best friend?

I don't know yet what this knot is trying to tell me, but I can't even bring myself to open the dossier, such is my level of shame. I do hope there are no consequences to my actions. After all, what danger could there be in giving one name to a perfect angel in year eleven form? Please tell me I'm just being paranoid.

Number of views: 47,376   **Likes:** 2,573

SURVEILLANCE REPORT

by Trainee Agent

Belle Pepper

Mission successful - target has received dossier and named The Fish. According to my research, and based on activities at Colpepper Hall School, the next heist is likely to be in London. An opportunity to catch The Fish red-handed. See you there.

Dearest Mia,

You never know, having Michael Chimaera involved may well have its uses, you'll see. So I'm pleased he's agreed to help with the petition, but I'm sorry this has led to a falling out between you and Shanice. Remember, there's always more than one way to get results (as I've just described in my latest article, ***Growing Problem of Manure: Farmers Told To Step On It***), and even if you're no longer including her petition, maybe you could find a way to spread Shanice's message? You have more power than you realize.

You've worked so hard on your petition and on planning this trip, I'm sure it will go brilliantly. And even if it doesn't quite go as you expect, it will all turn out for the best. I'm sure you'll have lots to tell me afterwards.

Must go – am paddle-boarding down the Hudson and don't want my phone to get wet! XXX

Kat B. | Freelance journalist for science and nature | fjsn.net
Sent from my phone

Lost *Mona Lisa* Doomed to Remain Lost For Ever?

By Gerta Lowdaviss
The Daily News

As the search for *The Lost Mona Lisa* enters its final week, it is looking increasingly doubtful that the painting will ever be returned. The jewel in the royal family's art collection will never grace their walls again – and no one will benefit from the £25 million reward.

In touching scenes, primary schools from around the country have been sending in possible replacement pictures to Buckingham Palace – many based on *The Mona Lisa*, including one sent by Wrawby School, measuring over two metres in length, and made up entirely of pupils' handprints… READ MORE

View comments

Related Topics

| Art | Royal Family | Mona Lisa | Culture |

_____

Dear Granny,

I now have my NEW glasses, which, everyone keeps telling me, look REALLY GOOD on me. But I really miss the ones you gave me because it turns out I do quite like standing out from the crowd and they were definitely eye-catching! Mr Rothering has now STOPPED calling me Dame Edna, which I kind of miss, as it was a nice little joke between him and me, even if I still don't really understand it. Other people may think these new ones look good but, with their clunky frame, they really hurt the sides of my head.

Meanwhile, it seems that mosquitoes have infested the school as well as crickets; I swear I can hear a high-pitched buzzing wherever I go.

I wanted to talk to Shanice about now being "GLASSES TWINS", but she's still annoyed with me. Thankfully, she HAS to come to London still because she's in the orchestra. But it turns out perfect Belle Pepper plays the clarinet and has suddenly joined too! So she's also coming with us to London – grrr, why do I find her so irritating?

And speaking of being irritating, Jake hasn't even been bothering to

LOOK at me these last few days, even though he should be all over my new glasses. Surely he KNOWS they're from MC Glasses? Where's his outrage? Why isn't he telling me that I'm being mind-controlled?

Whatever. I don't care.

Mum and Dad seem to be in a really good mood this week, and it's so lovely to see them happy. Mum has finished whatever sculpture she's been creating in the garage, and Dad has been really studying the plans for the National Gallery; I think, because it's such 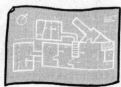 a HUGE gallery, he's determined that no one in the group gets lost. You can tell they're looking forward to London, although I have heard them talking about "getting this last one out of the way", whatever that means. I guess, even if they don't love galleries, they've been going to them for me, and that's enough.

Everything else at school feels like it's coming to an end for the Christmas holidays. We finished our Greek project in history and Mr Carpsucker was pleased with my essay on the Trojan Horse. Although he only gave me an A this time, which felt a bit of a let-down after my A+++++ before. I wonder why he liked my other project so much more. I invited him along to London with us, but he said he was looking forward to welcoming the group back after the trip and for a successful conclusion to the whole episode.

Love, *Mia*

Mr and Mrs Berghler,

Nearly there now. Just one last job. You've done so well. Your starfish is safe. I'm so sorry to have forced you into this. I'm not really a bad person. But if you don't succeed with the last heist, I will have to do something very unpleasant to your starfish, and I fear it would get very messy, so do bear that in mind. Get the last picture and bring it to Colpepper Hall School on your return from London.

Dear Granny,

I'm waiting around to get up on to the plinth and am just taking a moment to email you because EVERYTHING IS GOING HORRIBLY WRONG.

Dad put my tuba case with the other instrument cases under the coach, but somehow I had forgotten to put the tuba inside the case! So I was stuck with the tuba on my lap for the whole trip down to London – and it's really heavy. Mum and Dad waved goodbye; they were going to drive separately and meet us in London, since they had to bring Mum's papier-mâché sculpture.

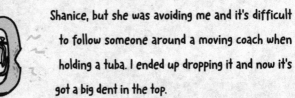

I was hoping to use the journey to patch things up with Shanice, but she was avoiding me and it's difficult to follow someone around a moving coach when holding a tuba. I ended up dropping it and now it's got a big dent in the top.

Without Shanice to talk to, I tried to get Jake's attention, but he also seems to be avoiding me. He also seems to be avoiding Belle Pepper now too, though, so it's not all bad news.

THEN we got to London, and the plan was to set up the orchestra at the bottom of the plinth while Mum and Dad prepared the top of the plinth with Mum's creation - but it turns out that what Mum had made out of papier-mâché was A GIANT *STARFISH* .

A GIANT STARFISH!

REALLY?

After all we've been through and with Mum KNOWING how important this trip is for me - she makes a GIANT STARFISH .

And, I mean, it's really huge. Like, a full-grown man could fit in each of the five arms.

So I got really upset and *may* have shouted at Mum.

Then Dad got cross with me and told me that they were only doing ALL OF THIS for the good of the family. And THEN he pointed out that Mum's massive papier-mâché sculpture wasn't actually a *STARFISH* - it was the five-pointed thing from the school logo.

Ah.

Whoops.

I mean. It does look quite starfishy.

BUM .

So my best friends are ignoring me, I've dented my tuba and I need to find Mum to apologize but both her and Dad have now disappeared off somewhere, and it is time for me to get up on the cherry picker with Michael Chimaera MP so we can do our photo shoot and big announcement on the *Fourth Plinth*, next to the big stupid papier-mâché STARFISH that is not a STARFISH.

Can this day get any worse?

Love, Mia

Dear Granny,

So I've just finished my BIG MOMENT on the top of the Fourth Plinth and IT WAS GREAT!

I got up there and was given a microphone so I could talk about my PETITION for persuading the government to fund arts education properly. I looked down (wow, that plinth is a LONG WAY up) and saw massive crowds standing all around. It was SUCH a special moment, and I felt a big sense of pride that my PETITION my little petition – had grown into something that was getting proper attention and was actually going to be debated in Parliament.

Even though I wanted to take my time, I could sense Michael Chimaera next to me, just itching to get his hands on the microphone. I managed to pick out Mr Rothering and Miss Tench in the crowd below, but I couldn't see Mum or Dad anywhere. I knew they had to be around somewhere. Them and my not-quite-friends.

I had the microphone. I had the power – it was MY MOMENT!

And I knew what I needed to say.

So, I started off by introducing myself and saying that I needed to say sorry to Mum, and I thanked everyone for making such a big effort to help me with my PETITION and to support the trip to London. And then I used the publicity and plinth and microphone to highlight something that wouldn't be debated in parliament – Shanice's PETITION!

So I told the crowd, which was getting bigger and bigger, about my friend Shanice and our project at Colpepper Hall School and all about Lord Colpepper and how horrible he actually was and that I agree with my friend that we should stop paying tribute to bad people from history.

But that's about as far as I got because Michael Chimaera MP then grabbed the mic off me and got all the attention on to him – but I'd definitely managed to make things better, because when the cherry picker took us back down (which took ages and was really awkward because Michael Chimaera was REALLY annoyed with me), Shanice was waiting to give me a big hug. SORTED!

I had been hoping Mum and Dad would also be waiting with hugs, but still no sign of them.

Now all that remains today is for us to get into the National Gallery and find the final painting from Lord Colpepper's collection – Rubens's *Splayed Corpse* – but unless Mum and Dad turn up soon, they're going to miss it.

Love, *Mia*

From: MiaB@StarfishInstructions.net   ☰ ×
To: KBerg55@fjsn.net
Date: 19 December
Subject: REALLY AWFUL NEWS

Mum and Dad have been ARRESTED!!!

Can you believe it?

Me and the rest of the group had gone into the
National Gallery to find the Rubens picture and
apparently someone had reported something
suspicious about the GIANT PAPIER-MÂCHÉ

STARFISH on top of the Fourth Plinth (although, of course – NOT A
STARFISH) so the POLICE were called and swooped in, and there, INSIDE
the giant starfish-which-is-not-a-starfish, were Mum and Dad!

I really wanted to go up and hug them but I couldn't get near them
and I wasn't even allowed to TALK to them as they were being dragged off

by the police. They looked so confused and upset
by the whole situation, which is never how you
want to see your parents. Can you believe it?
The police suspect Mum and Dad of being art
thieves! Somehow annoying Belle Pepper had
completely managed to muscle in on the action

– couldn't she just mind her own business? She was laughing and joking
with the authorities like they were best friends.

I TRIED to explain that Mum had MADE the giant starfish-which-is-not-a-starfish and they had probably both got trapped in there when trying to assemble all the different parts at the top of the Fourth Plinth, which must have been really tricky. The officer I spoke to looked **_very dubious_** about my story and said *he* believed it was "a classic Trojan Horse attempt to access the secret tunnel to the National Gallery from the plinth".

YEAH RIGHT.

As if that explanation is more believable than mine.

Whoever would be so RIDICULOUS as to attempt an art heist by hiding in a papier-mâché sculpture of a non-starfish?

Mr Rothering was super helpful about the whole thing and offered to stay behind and sort everything out for my parents, while Miss Tench *insisted* that the coach needed to get back to Colpepper and *insisted* I really had to get on it. So I've had to leave my parents UNDER ARREST IN LONDON.

This trip has turned out to be a NIGHTMARE.

Love, *Mia*

PS We didn't even get to see the Rubens picture because, when we got to the place in the gallery wall where it should have been, there was a little note which read:

> **Peter Paul Rubens**
> *Splayed Corpse* (1640)
> Sketch
> Charcoal on paper
>
> *As part of the Take One schools project,*
> *this work of art is currently on loan from*
> *the National Gallery to Colpepper Hall*
> *School, Colpepper.*

Are you KIDDING me? The last of the five pictures from Lord Colpepper's collection was back at the school ALL ALONG?

EYE FOR TRUTH

by Jake Janowski

That's what the knot in my stomach was trying to tell me: I was being BLINDED BY LOVE. I have been played like a clarinet. How could I have been such a fool?

I've just seen the parents of my best friend being carted off by the police and it was COMPLETELY MY FAULT. Not only that, they were caught in some weird papier-mâché creation, which tells me for certain that they can't possibly be The Fish. The Fish would definitely NOT let themselves be caught in some weird papier-mâché creation.

So I was wrong.

And I've betrayed my friend.

But I was *so sure* I was right about The Fish's identity. I mean, it all made so much sense, didn't it?

And if they aren't The Fish, who is? Who has been stealing the Lord Colpepper paintings – and why?

From: KBerg55@fjsn.net   ☰ ×
To: MiaB@StarfishInstructions.net
Date: 19 December
Subject: Just a thought

Dearest Mia,

How terrible! Surely your parents are not involved in stealing art! But, you know, it's the most curious thing: I've been reading about recent thefts of paintings, and artworks have been stolen from the same galleries you've been visiting! And which paintings have gone missing? Why, the pictures from Colpepper Hall! Four of the five have been targeted. It's almost like *someone* is trying to get them back together. Didn't you see the newspaper reports?

And if the fifth picture is back at school, does anyone know exactly where it is? Perhaps if the final picture is found, all will become clear.

What a mystery! Aren't you curious? If only there was *someone* you could talk to about this. Is the idea of someone targeting and stealing the pictures from Colpepper Hall completely *bonkers*? XXX

Kat B. | Freelance journalist for science and nature | fjsn.net
Sent from my phone

Dear Granny,

You are so WISE. I was right to email you so much because you give really good advice and you properly read and remember what I tell you. THANK YOU!

After receiving your last email, I sat here on the coach thinking about those Lord Colpepper pictures and I saw what you meant about it actually being *rather suspicious* that someone had been going after them. Maybe it WAS too much of a coincidence, I started to think. But SURELY Mum and Dad could not be involved. They MUST be innocent. I have to prove it somehow and get them released.

I *thought* about talking to Shanice about this, but then it struck me...

Maybe, even if it DID sound BONKERS, it could still be TRUE – so, after that, there was only one person I needed: my WILD CONSPIRACY-THEORIST FRIEND JAKE!

I thought it was going to take AGES to persuade him to help me, but as soon I started to say something, he immediately burst into tears and claimed everything was his fault! Do you know, *he* had been thinking that my parents were The Fish. THE FISH! That was the famous art thief the security guard in Cardiff was talking about!

How could Jake believe Mum and Dad have anything to do with stealing art? He can't really believe my parents were somehow involved in the theft of all the pictures reported in the newspapers, can he? He's totally blaming himself for their arrest. What nonsense! It seems like he was basing his ENTIRE theory on the fact that StarfishInstructions.net contains an ANAGRAM of ART HEISTS. How loopy is that?

Not **EVERYTHING** is an anagram, I told him!

Once he calmed down, we came up with a plan. When the coach gets back to Colpepper and everyone has gone home, WE'RE GOING TO BREAK INTO SCHOOL AND FIND THE LAST PICTURE. Maybe then we'll find out just what has been going on. I have a sneaking suspicion I know where to find it – and Jake agrees.

I know that sounds really exciting and everything, but I just wish I FELT better. I've got a MASSIVE headache.

Wish us luck!

Love, *Mia*

From: MiaB@StarfishInstructions.net ≡ ✕
To: KBerg55@fjsn.net
Date: 20 December
Subject: FREEDOM!

Dear Granny,

MUM and DAD are FREEEEEEEEEE!!! They're on their way back from London as I write this email.

And it's all thanks to me and Jake.

Once the coach dropped us off and the others had gone home, we tried to break into the school. Turns out that was SUPER EASY because SOMEONE was there already – and that someone was...

Mr Carpsucker!

He looked rather surprised to see *us*. He was wearing gloves, which at first I thought was because of his dirt-phobic super tidiness – but then I suddenly wasn't so sure, because we found him in the school's entrance hall with...

Da Da Dahhhhhh!

The FOUR pictures from Lord Colpepper's collection, which he'd hung on the walls in the Dome Area.

So *HE* was behind all the art thefts!

Anyway, when he saw us, he asked where my parents were, which I guess is fair enough, as it was REALLY late and we shouldn't have been at school. He got a panicked look in his eyes and ran his fingers through his hair, which messed it up. As he smoothed down his hair, he muttered about "Gathering all the skeleton keys" and "Needing the Rubens to spell out CRYPT". Then he just started sobbing: "When they're all in place, all will be revealed."

Whatever Mr Carpsucker had been doing there, he had clearly been expecting someone to deliver the picture by Rubens to him. Those five pictures from Lord Colpepper's collection were being brought back together for *some* reason.

Jake was really good with Mr Carpsucker and spoke to him really soothingly, so he'd calm down a bit, and then I explained that the Rubens picture was somewhere in the school. At that, Mr Carpsucker jumped up and GRABBED me and said we had to find that last picture.

Wow – he looked so desperate.

I was about to tell him where I suspected the Rubens to be when JAKE butted in and said he was sure it would be in the art department – and that he just happened to have a key. I was quite annoyed about this because,

while wild theories ARE Jake's thing, it doesn't mean that *other* people can't have ideas. And back on the coach, I  thought he'd agreed with me about *my* theory about the location of the final picture! I was sulking about this while I followed Jake and Mr Carpsucker to the art department, where Jake unlocked the door ... and shoved Mr Carpsucker inside!

BRILLIANT.

Jake locked the door back up pretty quickly and there were all kinds of screams and sounds of thrashing and smashing. He TOTALLY dealt with Mr Carpsucker!

We rushed to the biology lab and there, on the wall, was what I was looking for - turns out a *Splayed Corpse* is another name for a skeleton with all its skin pinned back. An actual real sketch by RUBENS had been hanging in our biology department all this time! I guess someone in the school office hadn't understood what the Take One programme from the museum was all about, and just assumed this PRICELESS RUBENS SKETCH was meant as a teaching aid in the lab! Now, if that doesn't tell you the dire need for more arts education in this country, I don't know what does...

We took the picture back to the entrance hall and put it up on the wall in the space that Mr Carpsucker had left for it, and ... nothing.

Nothing happened!

I'm not sure what I'd been expecting, but from Mr Carpsucker's mutterings, it had sounded like *something* would happen once the Rubens was in place. And I was thinking to myself, *What had he meant about the crypt?*

And then I saw it.

The order he'd hung the paintings was:

1) Cranach the Elder

2) Rubens

3) Brueghel the Younger

4) Poussin

5) Turner

The names were spelling out CRYPT!

But something didn't seem right. We were missing something.

And then Jake said something very wise. Something BRILLIANT. Something a very CLEVER person told him. On a coach. About an hour before.

He said, "Not everything is an ANAGRAM" – and I saw he was right.

Of course, the names couldn't be an anagram of Crypt because Brueghel starts with a B, not a Y. And if Younger had counted, why hadn't Elder, which would have spelled Erypt – which is not a word!

We took the five pictures off the wall, laid them on the floor and stood over them. I just kept thinking to myself, *We must be missing something.* They were all slightly different sizes and different weights. They were different materials and from different times – there was no obvious sensible order to put them in.

We didn't have time to hang the five different pictures all the different ways that five paintings could be hung because that's, like, a-hundred-and-twenty different ways. I feared we did not have that much time.

What was I MISSING?

I stared so hard at the paintings, I swear my eyes started to blur even

WITH my glasses on - and all I could see then was the weird marking on the floor, fanning out from the bust of Lord Colpepper. The more I looked at those markings, the more it looked like a hand (OK, maybe Jake was right from the start about the school logo shape), with each spindly finger stretching out to the five parts of the wall where the five pictures should hang. And then I caught sight of the motto on the base of the bust: SUCCESS IS AT OUR FINGERTIPS.

And then it struck me!

I knew exactly what was missing! I had studied these pictures. I knew them better than anyone.

All the skeletons in the pictures have one finger missing - and those missing digits together make up one hand - a hand that maybe, just maybe, was the right order for hanging the pictures! Working as quickly as possible, we matched up the paintings with the floor markings, according to which finger was missing in each painting and, just as we hung the fifth and final painting in place, something gave a loud *clunk*.

Suddenly, the bust of Lord Colpepper started to rotate slowly and sink into the floor. With each creaking turn, a section of the floor lowered too, creating five huge, deep steps downwards - separated by the weird floor finger markings and scattered with random pieces of paper. At this point, Jake had a big "I thought as much" smile on his face. It was incredible, Granny; there we were at the top of a big spiral staircase down into ... *who knows?*

Like the motto said, success really was at our fingertips! REALLY ANNOYINGLY, just as we were about to climb down, we heard sirens and the screech of tyres from outside. POLICE! I have no idea who called them, but we realized we needed to go and explain the whole Mr-Carpsucker-locked-in-the-art-department situation before we got into *real* trouble.

When Jake unlocked the art department for the police, I could see exactly why Mr Carpsucker had been so freaked out: the rooms were full of LIZARDS, COCKROACHES and CRICKETS!

How weird is that?

The police were asking A LOT of questions while they were trying to calm down Mr Carpsucker enough to take him away. I'm not sure Jake helped matters much by going on about our headteacher being a lizard man. Jake can be SO EMBARRASSING.

Finally, Mr Scales turned up, bleary-eyed, and was able to explain it all. It turns out that Mr Scales's grand plan for raising money for the school in order to save the east wing from becoming a car park was to breed CHAMELEONS – what a BONKERS idea! That was never going to work! So when we locked Mr Carpsucker in there in the dark, he ended up knocking over quite a lot of the tanks and then found himself being crawled over by things he could only imagine.

When I last saw him, he was still trying to comb his hair with his hands cuffed behind his back - but I'm not sure he'll ever feel neat or clean again after the whole being-trapped-with-reptiles-and-insects experience.

The good news is that the police sent word to London to free Mum and Dad. They were quite certain they'd got their man for those heists, as Mr Carpsucker had had all the stolen Colpepper pictures with him when we'd arrived.

The not-so-good news is that when we returned to the Dome Area with the police and climbed down the big steps, all they led to was a series of huge rooms - completely empty! I was sure there'd be some kind of treasure hidden down there. After all, someone had gone to a lot of trouble to hide the space - and Mr Carpsucker had gone to a lot of trouble to find the space again.

Even though I was disappointed, Mr Scales was delighted! Here was a whole new set of rooms that the school could use - a new art department! I've never seen him look so pleased - he even SMILED!

So even if we didn't find any treasure, we've got the credit for finding the crypt. The east wing can be demolished, Colpepper can get its new car park - and the school will have lovely new rooms to use, even if they are underground and a bit dark and damp. Well, you can't have everything!

Love, *Mia*

Dearest Mia,

What an exciting adventure!

I'm so pleased you thought to get Jake involved; I *knew* you were still friends. And how marvellous that you managed to prove your parents' innocence. In fact, look at everything you've managed to achieve over the last few weeks: not only have you solved the art department problem for your headteacher, you've also presented a petition that will hopefully put a stop to planned cuts in arts education. I told you everything would work out for the best.

Maybe it's time for me to plan a trip to Colpepper? I've been working so hard lately, it's time I took a break. And after all your parents have been through recently, I have a feeling we all might get along better now. XXX

Kat B. | Freelance journalist for science and nature | fjsn.net
Sent from my phone

Hey M,

Have you SEEN the news? Can you believe it? Surely too much of a coincidence? Want to investigate?

JJ

J,

Just because SOME of your theories have

proved correct, doesn't mean there's anything

suspicious about this. Calm down and have a

Wagon Wheel! :)

Mx

Lost Mona Lisa Found
– And Just In The Nick Of Time

By Gerta Lowdaviss
The Daily News

Call off the search! *The Lost Mona Lisa* **was discovered yesterday in the back cupboard of the local Colpepper optician's by Michael Chimaera, MP.**

"I'm amazed," said Mr Chimaera. "I never open that cupboard, but, due to the excellent reporting on the search for the painting and encouraging us all to leave no stone unturned, I felt it was my civic duty to play my part and search my premises – and I'm so glad I did!"

This journalist caught a glimpse of the freshly found painting, and it certainly looks to be the real deal. Even better than the Louvre's version, for sure!

The royal family are sending over a team of experts to verify the painting, and then it will be taken back to the Royal Collection, to be enjoyed for years to come.

And, of course, there is the small matter of the £25 million reward. Mr Chimaera has said that he would like to use some of the money to help glorify Lord Colpepper's legacy in the local area and has, most kindly, already pledged £5,000 to Colpepper Hall School to repair the nose on the bust of Lord Colpepper. Such a generous donation from our local benefactor and Colpepper's newest millionaire, Michael Chimaera!

View comments

Related Topics

Art   Royal Family   Mona Lisa   Culture

EYE FOR TRUTH

by Jake Janowski

I see I've lost many of my followers and, from your comments, many of you have rudely expressed your disappointment in EYE FOR TRUTH. For what? Because I was brave enough to admit I was wrong!

Is that not allowed?

Does everyone have to be right ALL the time? Is no one allowed to change their mind? Or admit a mistake?

Well, for my true, loyal readers, there's still much to uncover.

Let's look at the nonsense reported this morning in the newspaper...

WHAT? Are people actually BELIEVING this nonsense?

And how can my parents publish this rubbish saying that £5,000 out of £25 million is GENEROUS?

So I may have been wrong about *some* things, but let's look at the evidence, people:

Michael Chimaera just magically "finds" *The Lost Mona Lisa* in a cupboard in the MC Glasses building? A day after a crypt is mysteriously discovered under Colpepper Hall? Under somewhere that had belonged to his *relative*? This is all *very suspicious.*

Surely I can't be the only one seeing a link between the goings-on at school last night and this sudden announcement of *The Lost Mona Lisa's* discovery?

Who knew that ME and MY BEST FRIEND were going to break into school to try to solve the problem of the stolen pictures from Lord Colpepper's collection?

NO ONE, that's who.

And WE didn't ring the police that night – so who did?

Bear with me here: WHAT was Mia wearing when we talked about our plans? WHAT was Mia wearing when we were solving the puzzle of the Colpepper paintings?

Her new glasses from MC Glasses, that's what!

So, what if there is something dodgy about MC Glasses after all? What if Michael Chimaera was using the glasses to SPY on people? What if Michael Chimaera called the police to cause a distraction so he got to search the newly discovered crypt first?

You know I'm right.

And not just about the glasses – look at my theory about Mr Scales. Was Mr Scales a lizard man? Well, no, I'll grant you that. But he WAS doing something weird and suspicious and lizardy. And who saw all this?

ME! I did.

And so what if I was wrong about The Fish? There's definitely something FISHY going on in Colpepper, what with all those Abrahams gang people AND Mr Carpsucker being arrested. Were they all working for Michael Chimaera? Could Michael Chimaera be The Fish? Well, come to think of it, he *was* a pupil at Colpepper Hall School and his name is a kind of fish (I've just looked it up). Was I suspecting the wrong people the whole time?

I'm afraid I can't bring myself to look in the dossier of evidence – it's a guilty reminder of my betrayal – but I will make sure I do all I can to help my best friend.

Hey M,

Don't believe me - that's OK. But I think I have evidence of who The Fish is - and I want you to be the person to look at it. Can we meet?

JJ

From: MiaB@StarfishInstructions.net

To: KBerg55@fjsn.net

Date: 22 December

Subject: So long, Seabert

Dear Granny,

The STRANGEST thing has happened. SEABERT has suddenly REAPPEARED!

The police brought him to us this morning!

And the WEIRDEST thing is that Mum and Dad are talking about finding a new place for him to live, somewhere with lots of sea-creature friends for him! So, look out, Colpepper Aquarium! It looks like you're getting a new STAR attraction.

Funnily enough, I will miss SEABERT, but I think Mum and Dad have got used to him not being around. Do you know, when they got back from being arrested in London, they hugged me SO tight, I thought my head would pop off. Either that, or I'd faint from the smell – because, apparently, getting trapped in a papier-mâché sculpture and then spending the night in a police cell makes people REALLY stinky! While I was worried about them, they were SUPER worried about me. They missed me! So it is just going to be the three of us now. We can always visit SEABERT – between trips to art galleries, of course.

Tomorrow there's a big event in Colpepper town square at four p.m. Apparently the experts from the Royal Collection have finished assessing *The Lost* MONA LiSA (although maybe they should call it *The FOUND* MONA LiSA now?!), and there's going to be this big celebration with the painting being displayed publicly before being taken back to Buckingham Palace and Mr Chimaera receiving his big cheque – lucky him!

I've promised Jake I'll see him there, and apparently he's developed YET ANOTHER THEORY and this time he even thinks he's got real evidence! He seems to think it's MASSIVELY suspicious that Michael Chimaera just happened to find the painting in his building just after the crypt was discovered in Colpepper Hall School. But we have to trust our local MP, don't we?

After all, we spread false rumours about Michael Chimaera before and that did not go well.

Love, *Mia*

Dear Granny,

Wow! Just back from *The* MONA LiSA celebrations in town and they were a lot more exciting - or even EXPLOSIVE - than I thought they were going to be!

This morning had already been exciting enough as me, Mum and Dad took SEABERT off to his new home at Colpepper Aquarium. The aquarium is delighted to have a new, famous exhibit and we were all photographed for the *Colpepper Online Gazette*. With such a prized STARFISH now in its collection, the aquarium is concerned over security and has asked "Starfish Instructions" to help out with a new alarm system - but the aquarium will have to get in line because Mum and Dad have been swamped with requests for work from galleries desperate to replace their proven-to-be-unreliable Verisafe Alarm 3000s. Yay!

This afternoon, when I met up with Jake for the Mona Lisa celebrations, he immediately knocked my glasses off my face, which was odd behaviour, even for Jake.

THAT IS NOT COOL AND DEFINITELY NOT OK!

But, however much I complained, Jake wouldn't give them back to me. I'd never seen him so determined. He was adamant that something was up with the glasses.

Oh, for goodness' sake! But, that's Jake – I guess he'll always have some cockamamie idea or other. Love Jake, love his theories!

The royal family were clearly taking security for the painting VERY SERIOUSLY and had sent a massive security team to the event. It was a good job too; I'm sure the WHOLE of Colpepper turned up to see the painting. Everyone was queuing to see it, positioned on a special plinth outside MC Glasses. The funny thing is, do you know who I thought I'd seen in the crowd?

YOU!

Even without my glasses, I was *convinced* it was you!

I called your name, but I must have been mistaken because you didn't turn around – or maybe you didn't hear me because Michael Chimaera was standing on the podium and going on and on and on about how great Lord Colpepper was and how the millions of pounds will help him regain some of his family's former glory and blah, blah, blah.

Then, all of a sudden, there was a very loud KA-BOOM! Someone had set off fireworks as part of the celebration, and the crowd turned to watch, their eyes on the sky as it lit up. As I wasn't really able to watch the fireworks (oooh – slightly blurry lights in the sky – really exciting, thanks, Jake!), I took the opportunity to slip closer to the painting. Thankfully, my close-up vision works just fine, so while everyone else was watching the fireworks, I got to spend time, on my own, looking at a masterpiece. And it *is* a masterpiece. The Mona Lisa's skin was luminous, her smile was teasing and subtle, and there, just under her nose, was a very tiny FISH.

A FISH?

I pointed this out to the security team, and all hell broke loose.

The "experts" were called back and started to talk in a panicky way. Even though

they had been CONVINCED that the painting was authentic just moments before, now, having had the tiny fish pointed out to them BY ME, they said it was a FORGERY – and not just ANY forgery, apparently the tiny fish is a sign that it was done by the art thief called ... wait for it: The Fish!

And then Jake got involved – shouting, **"I knew it! Michael Chimaera is The Fish!"**

Bloomin' Jake – always jumping in with his theories!

But maybe he was right. Maybe Michael Chimaera – AKA The Fish – was trying to claim the £25 million reward by giving a near-perfect copy of the painting to the royal family. But, judging by what Michael Chimaera did next, I'm not so sure.

When Mr Chimaera saw what was going on, he **COMPLETELY** lost it. (Jake was finding this all so entertaining that he kindly gave me back

my glasses so I could witness it too!) Michael Chimaera, when he spotted the fish in the fake painting, ripped the painting off the plinth and started smashing it around. He was shouting, "It was real. It was definitely real. The family rumours were true. They were definitely true!"

And with that, Michael Chimaera flung the painting...

I ducked.

Jake ducked.

Everyone ducked.

And the painting sailed into MC Glasses and smashed into the back wall, which splintered and fell over – it was just a thin, wooden panel, really – revealing hundreds of small screens! You should have seen Mr Chimaera's face when he realized what he'd done; it was like a naughty child being caught licking the chocolate spread jar!

Jake and I rushed into the shop to have a better look at the screens, and they looked to be all different views of Colpepper. Not only that, there was one screen that looked to be showing EXACTLY what I was seeing!

MICHAEL CHIMAERA has been planting mini cameras in people's glasses, so he could keep tabs on us!!

HOW MESSED UP IS THAT?

    Jake is now very smug, going on about having suspected Mr Chimaera THE WHOLE TIME, which is not strictly true. Lying about finding a painting and spying on people is very different from mind control, but Jake still sees it as a win and, as his best friend, I'm happy to let him believe that.

Love, *Mia*

PS Jake handed me a Wagon Wheel and a "dossier of evidence" about The Fish – as if I care (about the dossier, I mean. I definitely care about the Wagon Wheel)! He says he doesn't want it because it's a symbol of his betrayal and blindness (whatever that means). I guess now Michael Chimaera has been caught it's no longer needed anyway. I'll probably just ditch it – but maybe after one sneak peek. It can't do any harm.

Finder Of Mona Lisa Found To Be A Fraud!

By Gerta Lowdaviss
The Daily News

Local optician and MP admits to spying on and lying to the public

Michael Chimaera is under arrest following the discovery of hundreds of screens at MC Glasses, all linked up to tiny cameras on glasses worn by his many customers in the town of Colpepper. When asked why he went to such lengths to spy on his customers, Mr Chimaera explained that he had spent his lifetime looking for clues – any clues at all – that would lead him to *The Lost Mona Lisa*. Due to a family secret, Michael Chimaera knew that *The Lost Mona Lisa* was somewhere hidden in Colpepper Hall. He maintains that he found the *real **Lost Mona Lisa*** in the Crypt of Colpepper Hall School on December 19.

If what Mr Chimaera claimed is true, the world's most famous painting was stolen two-hundred years ago by Lord Colpepper himself – from a Christmas party held by his friend King George IV in 1822.

Mr Chimaera denies using a forgery to try to trick the royal family into passing over the £25 million reward, but the evidence is stacked against him. Police say that the forged painting containing the fish – now in shreds as pictured, the complicated heists and the use of stooges

and diversions all add up to prove that Mr Chimaera is in fact the most infamous art thief of all: The Fish.

And, in an astonishing twist, the real, true and definitely verified *Lost Mona Lisa* has been ***anonymously returned*** to the royal family! The painting's whereabouts over the last two-hundred years will remain a mystery, but it is wonderful news for the royal family to have the painting home where it belongs. The painting's unnamed saviour did not wish to claim the £25 million reward for themselves but instead requested that the majority of the reward goes to arts education for secondary school pupils, with £3 million going to Colpepper Hall School to establish a new art department – on the condition that Colpepper Hall School is renamed, using a name chosen by the pupils themselves.

View comments

Related Topics

| Art | Royal Family | Mona Lisa | Culture |

TOP SECRET

Compiled by

Agent Carrot*

of the

International
Espionage Agency

Dossier of Evidence Detailing
Known Activities of the

Infamous Art Thief
Known as

The Fish

* Assisted by
Trainee Agent Belle Pepper

To the Royal Family,

Aren't you sick of the Louvre getting all of the glory over their version of The Mona Lisa by Leonardo da Vinci? Aren't you sick of people thinking that da Vinci only painted one version of The Mona Lisa? Aren't you sick of the idea that your copy, which academics believed to be the superior of the two, is known as The Lost Mona Lisa? Wouldn't it be wonderful if it became The Found Mona Lisa? Think of the national pride that would be restored if it could be located. Think of the crowds, the merchandise, the money!

Well, I am delighted to report that The Lost Mona Lisa still exists! Please see the below note which proves the painting lies hidden, waiting to be discovered. You are probably aware that it is nearly two-hundred years since the jewel in your collection went missing. With the right incentive, such as a generous reward, I am certain the painting could be returned in time for the two hundredth anniversary of the theft.

Yours sincerely,

Deirdre Demoiselle

A concerned citizen, I am — and a very private one. Please do not release my name to the press.

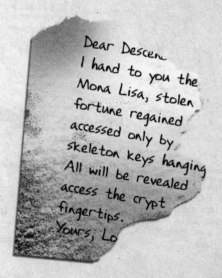

Dear Descen
I hand to you the
Mona Lisa, stolen
fortune regained
accessed only by
skeleton keys hanging
All will be revealed
access the crypt
fingertips.
Yours, Lo

LANCE LING

Deborah Dab

PAULA PARORE

Barbara Burramundi

SUSPECTED ALIASES

MARY MUDSKIPPER

Nina Nase

SUSPECTED GALLERIES TARGETED

NATIONAL GALLERY OF MODERN ART BANGALURU, INDIA

WHITWORTH ART GALLERY MANCHESTER

TOKYO MUSEUM OF CONTEMPORARY ART

SEATTLE ART MUSEUM

Sir JOHN SOANES MUSEUM LONDON

ISABELLA STEWART GARDNER MUSEUM BOSTON

ACADEMIA GALLERY OF VENICE

FRANKFURT

VARIOUS GALLERIES TARGETED

MELBOURNE GALLERY OF VICTORIA

THE **FISH**

EVIDENCE

METHODS

DISGUISES

Dark blue, curly hair

Short + blond

Pink plaits

Knotted together stockings

Escaped on a speedboat/ gondola/ water-skis

Most unlikely getaway 'driver': sharks

Shaving foam covered security cameras

Replacing oxygen in guard room for laughing gas

SHARK

UNUSUAL GOINGS-ON in GALLERIES

SUSPECTED FISH ACTIVITY

MOUSE

New natural spring discovered under gallery

Guards suffering upset stomachs with anonymous gift of pufferfish sushi

N N O

Guards distracted by infestation of mice

FOR ME TO INTERFERE. I H
SCHEDULE OF ACTIVITIES (

There is definitely a use to copying great works of art

Having Michael Chimaera involved may well have its uses

MAKE A BIG NOISE

The Fourth Plinth

THOSE BLASTED GALL

E PLANNED AN EXTENSIVE
R THE NEXT FEW MONTHS.

The Trojan Horse is such an ingenious way to get into a tricky place!

I was Mary Mudskipper

IT'S ALL PART OF A BIGGER PLAN

I want to steal the world's most famous painting

MS WERE ALWAYS GOING OFF DURING OUR GALLERY VISITS

AUTHOR'S NOTE

When I first started thinking about writing a book about art heists, it quickly made sense to focus on the most famous painting in the world: *The Mona Lisa* by Leonardo da Vinci. Even if you have very little interest in art, chances are that you may have heard of, and might recognize, *The Mona Lisa*. Every day, visitors crowd in their thousands to see this painting, which is owned by the Louvre Museum in Paris, France. (In reality, even though it is a beautiful masterpiece, created by a man who was a true genius, it is disappointingly small and slightly dingy – but perhaps that's just my taste!)

I knew I wanted my story to be about a painting that had been missing for a long time, but *The Mona Lisa* did not actually meet this criteria, so I made up a second copy that belonged to the British royal family. A key joy of being a writer is being able to create a new reality for the purposes of a book! Inventing a second copy of *The Mona Lisa* is not really as far-fetched as it sounds, because it is thought that da Vinci created at least FOUR versions of *The Mona Lisa* over his lifetime: one is in the Prado Museum in Madrid, Spain, and others are in private collections.

When it comes to art, my entire book merges the real and imaginary. The galleries mentioned in the book all exist: National

Galleries, Scotland (in Edinburgh); Tate Liverpool; the National Museum of Wales in Cardiff; the National Gallery of Ireland (Dublin); the National Gallery in London; and all those listed in the dossier on The Fish. We are so lucky in this country for the quality of our national and regional galleries, many of which can be accessed for free, so everyone has the ability to see inspiring art collections. I could write a whole other book about the history of galleries and the amazing work these institutions do to engage with schools and the public (the *Fourth Plinth* project and the *Take One Picture* schools project really do exist, not to mention the workshops, sleepovers and many other exciting events that I have tried to give a small flavour of in this book).

While the figure of Lord Colpepper is imaginary, he is based on lots of historical figures, and paintings from the collections of rich old families in huge private mansions, such as Colpepper Hall, now hang in public art galleries (both in the United Kingdom and further afield). The "skeleton key" paintings do not exist – sadly I could not find five artists who lived before 1822 and who had conveniently painted pictures of skeletons with missing fingers! – so I used some "artistic license" and compromised. The skeleton key paintings are my invention but the five artists are all real and their work can be found in the five galleries Mia visits: you will find a Cranach in the National Galleries, Scotland, a Poussin in the National Museum of Wales and so on. Go on – visit for yourself and see!

ACKNOWLEDGEMENTS

This book is inspired by my lifelong interest in art and by having worked in museums and galleries for over a decade. My interest in art and history started with a family visit to Epworth Old Rectory in North Lincolnshire at around the age of seven. I can still remember being told about the staircase: wide and shallow to accommodate the fashion for women's voluminous dresses and men's tight trousers respectively. I became obsessed with the idea of living in an old, grand house in the past and wearing such fancy dresses, until my mum – rightly – pointed out that I would have been, at best, a scullery maid. My interest was not dimmed, however, and a school visit, at the age of eight, to Rufford Old Hall (where I learned about priest holes for the first time) virtually guaranteed that my future career would include something to do with art, history, or both. I am very grateful to the state schools I attended for broadening my horizons but, above all, I was incredibly lucky to have parents who recognized and encouraged my love of art and history.

I grew up at a time when art and creativity were central to the school curriculum and when university education was still free. Even with those advantages in place, the arts sector that

I found myself working in did not reflect the make-up of society and relied, instead, upon contacts, working initially for free and on pathetically low salaries. Without the "right" background, even the most talented or dedicated people found it hard to succeed.

Nowadays, the situation is even worse: despite institutions trying their hardest to broaden their appeal, both in terms of displays and events, and in terms of staffing, years of austerity and funding cuts are taking their toll. The pressure nowadays on the school day, on academic results and on budgets, means that the arts are being de-prioritized from a lower and lower age. Teachers do a brilliant job of trying to make sure as much creativity as possible is squeezed into the already over-stuffed curriculum but their time and resources are severely limited and, therefore, a future in the arts is often down to family support and finances. Potential art students do not want to be burdened with a lifetime of debt so end up choosing a different path. Increasingly, the arts are just for those who can afford to shoulder the debt, rather than based on anything related to talent.

Culture and the arts can be seen as frivolous – as not important – especially in the light of crises such as the pandemic or the climate emergency. But the arts touch so many aspects of our lives, from the type of television we watch to public art in our streets. Art and artists can start conversations, they can help solve problems, they can highlight plights and they help make the world a more beautiful place to live. Art is important and is, or should be, for everyone – it is a sign of a healthy society when all people can see themselves represented in the make-up of art institutions and in the work created. Although *How to Steal the Mona Lisa* is a light-hearted and funny art-heist caper of a book, there is a serious side to it and, if you look for them, these issues around the arts are covered here.

A massive thank you goes to my editor, the lovely Linas Alsenas, for his endless enthusiasm and support for this story. The whole team at Scholastic has done another fantastic job bringing this book to fruition and I am so lucky to be part of the Scholastic family. Special mentions go to Sarah for her eagle-eyed proofreading, and to Liam and Rachel, who have the headache of working out how to present the different types of communications! I am very grateful to be paired again with Jack Noel, whose amazing illustrations add so much energy and joy to the book.

Big thanks also go to Jo Williamson, my wonderful agent, and to my writing buddies who are always in the background with kind words and encouragement. Huge thanks to my friends and family, who gave massive amounts of support while I was writing this book and moving halfway up the country! And, finishing as I started, thank you to my parents for everything but especially for all the gallery visits, many of which helped inspire this book (I hope you weren't stealing paintings at the same time!) Mia's character was inspired, in part, by my mum's indefatigable approach to life, her sense of purpose and her avid letter-writing (and her terrible eyesight). I wish Mum had lived long enough to see me become a published author – it would have been the topic of a great many letters!

Also by Bethany Walker:

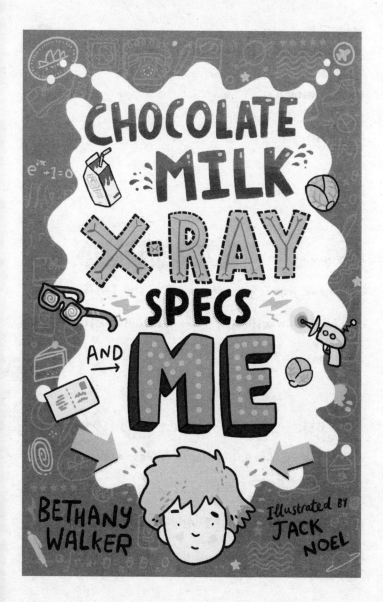

CHOCOLATE MILK X-RAY SPECS AND ME

BETHANY WALKER

Illustrated by JACK NOEL

Read on for an excerpt...

Mr and Mrs Spicer
The International Federation of Sprout Farmers
11353
Outer Castonga

March 30

Dear Mum and Dad,

Have you arrived in **OUTER CASTONGA** yet? I
hope your journey went well. I'm still GUTTED that I
couldn't come with you - are you ABSOLUTELY sure I
can't join you?

It sucks that you've had to go away so soon after
we've moved here. And who cares about farming
SPROUTS? I mean, what's the worst that
could happen: <u>no sprouts</u>? I wish you were still cabbage-
farming in Norfolk - at least then we were all together.

And why did you have to go away during the Easter holidays? There's NO ONE around to play with. You remember Ajay Coppertoe? Like us, he's only just moved here and we started school at the same time? Well, Ajay is the _one_ friend I've made since we moved here and he's on holiday with his dad, so the only person I've got to hang out with is Grandad. It's really boring.

I've been working hard on my Easter project. It was so nice of Lamont Riley to tell me about it. Lamont normally barely speaks to me. I can't believe I missed Mr Norbert's announcement to the class about the Easter project when I went off to the loo. Lamont _went out of his way_ to tell me all about the project. So nice of him! A 5,000 word essay on the history of pencils seems like a strange project to set – and it doesn't link with anything we've been learning at school – but at least it's something to do!

At EVERY meal, Grandad is feeding me sprouts. YUCK! Just because we get them free! I know you said, "A day without sprouts is a day without sunshine," but I'd be quite happy with a gazillion days of rain if it meant I didn't have to eat sprouts!

Better go. It's time for my chocolate milk. But Grandad always stirs the powder in. It's soooo much better how you do it - shaken, not stirred.

Love

Freddy

P.S. I tried to find **OUTER CASTONGA** on our globe but couldn't see it. It must be a very small country.